By the time Natasha got there, Tatiana was on the ground, straddling Gaia, her hands in a choking stranglehold around her neck. Gaia's arms were flailing, smacking haphazardly at Tatiana's face, shoulders, anywhere, just trying to get a grip on her to defend herself. But it was useless. Natasha approached and placed a foot squarely in the center of Gaia's chest, making it impossible for Gaia to move. Tatiana let go of her throat and held her flailing arms to the ground.

"Natasha," she wheezed, unable to get a decent breath with a boot on her chest. "Why are you doing this?"

"Stop the charade," Natasha scolded her. "I think you were expecting to see us. Perhaps not tonight, in this place, but when you took our gun, you knew we would come after you."

Don't miss any books in this thrilling series:

FEARLESS™

Available from SIMON PULSE

FEARLESS™

SHOCK

FRANCINE PASCAL

SIMON PULSE
New York   London   Toronto   Sydney   Singapore

First Simon Pulse edition May 2003

Copyright © 2003 by Francine Pascal

Cover copyright © 2003 by 17th Street Productions, an Alloy, Inc. company.

SIMON PULSE
An imprint of Simon & Schuster Children's Publishing Division
1230 Avenue of the Americas, New York, NY 10020

Produced by 17th Street Productions, an Alloy, Inc. company
151 West 26th Street
New York, NY 10001

Fearless™ is a trademark of Francine Pascal.

Printed in the United States of America
10 9 8 7 6 5 4 3 2 1

Library of Congress Control Number 2002117252
ISBN: 0-689-85764-0

To Isabelle Stevenson

Some mornings I wake up and everything seems okay. It's something my brain does. I suppose everyone's brain does it. You're in dreamland, and the wish fulfillment fairies take over and douse you in their bogus happy dust. Peek into your hidden desires and make you believe that you've satisfied them. Paint pictures that your eyes, flicking back and forth behind your closed lids, devour with an embarrassingly ravenous greed. And by the time you open your eyes, you're full of ill-gotten endorphins, convinced that all is well with the world.

Sometimes I can float there for thirty seconds, a minute, two minutes. I can will myself to believe I'm just a regular teenager whose biggest problem is figuring out how to sneak out after curfew. I can look at the sky outside my window and think, *Good morning, sunshine! Are we ready for another fabulous day?*

But reality always gets me in the end.

Before I can even wipe the boogers out of my eyes, I start to remember.

That's when the fairies take off. The minute they see my eyelids flicker, they start laughing like a bunch of punky eight-year-olds and take off out the window. And all the good feelings they gave me get slowly squished by the lead-and-tar mixture of the very real mess that is my life. I sink under the weight of reality. And pretty soon the bright colors of my dream fade to the dismal black-and-white of facts.

Fact one: Ed, my boyfriend up until last night, but more important, the person who's been my closest friend through all of this. . . well, he hates me. Wants to keep distance between us, where there used to be nothing but the best of friendships.

Fact two: Sam, my first love—as in the person you never fully get over—turns up just long enough to ruin things with Ed and then turns out to be a two-faced killer. Just like George Niven and everyone else I tried to trust.

And worst of all, fact three: My dad is missing. A particularly gut-wrenching fact that should make all boyfriend troubles irrelevant. He's out there somewhere, and nobody seems to know the first thing about how to find him. I might be his only hope. Which just makes me that much more of a target for whoever is trying to kill me.

Oh, yes. Trying to kill me. Shots fired, life in jeopardy. Someone actually wants to take this dismal life from me, and I'm damned if I'm going to let them. My father needs me too much.

For one brief moment I had everything I wanted: a family—two parents and a sister. A boyfriend. And I let myself believe it was mine, that those stupid dreams had really come true. And it all fell apart.

Note to self: Never fall for that one again.

Period.

End of story.

Beginning of day.

Rise and shine!

This was so
WEIRD. Like
a new reality
show: *When
Best* **human**
Friends
Go Bad. **obstacle**
They didn't
speak to
each other
like this.

GAIA MOORE EXITED THE BUILDING SHE

Electronic Dork Tool

lived in, on East Seventy-second Street, in a foul mood. She didn't even know where she was heading; she just knew she had to get out of that apartment and go somewhere, anywhere. It was stupid to stay in one place for long if her would-be killers—with or without the help of Sam—were looking for her. She wanted to search for her dad, but with nothing to go on, her energy just floated around in a hyper haze. It made her feel wired and weird.

To make matters worse, some asshole was letting his cell phone ring. Probably an idiot yuppie fresh from his morning workout getting a frantic call from the office asking what was going on with the Hooper account. Or a frazzled mom with two bratty kids who left her phone in the diaper bag and couldn't find it. Or some "boutique" dermatologist avoiding her needy patients jonesing for their Botox fix.

What Gaia couldn't understand was, why did people carry cell phones if they didn't want to answer them? And if they knew they were going to blow off a call, why not turn off the ringer and save everyone from having to hear that incessant, bleating whine? The worst part was, whoever the phone belonged to seemed to be following Gaia down the street. She glared at the people passing her, trying to shame who- ever it was into turning off that annoying ring, but it kept going and going. Jesus, it sounded like it was com- ing right from her own backpack. Who the hell. . . ?

Crap. It was Gaia's cell phone. She kept forgetting she was one of the wirelessly enhanced masses!

She dropped her backpack to the ground and quickly unzipped it, yanking the zipper up so that the grimy pack flopped against the ground. She spotted the cheerful silver phone in the dank recesses and reached in to get it, at which point it finally stopped.

Aaah. Sweet silence.

She checked the incoming-calls screen and saw that the phone number was for Dmitri's apartment. She hit the talk button twice and stood in the middle of the sidewalk, legs planted on either side of her open backpack, listening intently. She'd never get used to this tiny electronic dork tool. It clicked a few times, then beeped. She tried again, but the damn thing wouldn't connect. She waited to see if the little envelope would pop up—maybe he was leaving a message—but after about a minute and a half she real- ized that nothing was happening. Maybe Sam had signed her up for one of those low-rent plans.

Sam. As she closed up the phone, Gaia was disturbed to realize that her heart was thudding. Despite all evi- dence that he was a two-faced, double-crossing, wanna-be killer, there was still a part of her that just didn't get it. That wished he was calling. How dumb was that? The guy had given her instructions to meet him at a Ukranian church the night before, and as soon as she got there, *bam,* gunshots were headed straight for her gut. He had to be involved. He'd obviously been the willing bait to bring her there. But some small, idiotic part of her still felt a connection to the guy she had fallen for long ago.

The human heart was undeniably the stupidest organ in the body.

Forget it, she thought. *There's nowhere to go and nothing to do. I might as well go to school.*

Stuffing her nonworking phone into her backpack, she disappeared down the yawning maw of the subway tunnels. She'd try calling Dmitri again when she got to school.

Festive

GAIA WALKED UP THE CONCRETE STEPS to her high school in her usual state of bored irritation and inward concentration. Even if she were actually thinking about nothing more interesting than paper plates, it kept people from talking to her. But as she stepped through the wide metal doors, she stopped. Something was distinctly different.

There was a weird buzz in the air. Something undeniably festive was happening.

Gaia hated festive.

"What's going on?" she murmured to no one in particular.

"It's intramural week, silly," Megan shrieked. Megan was a particularly loathsome friend of Heather's. That is, she had been a friend of Heather's before Heather had gone blind from one of Loki's experiments and been whisked off to a hospital. Now she was a friend of Tatiana's—Gaia's roommate and almost stepsister had stepped into the part with barely a ripple—who looked surprisingly fresh, considering she'd been partying it up in Gaia's apartment just the night before. In fact, Megan was just as perky as she'd ever been. A cynical observer might even have said that Megan could barely tell the difference between Heather and Tatiana and didn't care which one was head of the proud crowd as long as Megan was among the top bananas. That FOH and FOT were all the same to Megan the Shallow. But that observer would have been a very, *very* cynical person.

"Intramural week." Gaia didn't state it in the form of a question, but Megan didn't let that stop her from expanding on her dementedly exciting news.

"I wouldn't expect you'd know about it," Megan said with a sigh. "I mean, Gaia, you're not exactly Miss School Spirit. But intramural week is when everybody forms different teams, and we play against each other."

"For what?" Gaia asked.

"For fun!" Megan squealed. "And trophies. But mostly for fun!" She moved in close, so close that their noses almost touched. Gaia caught a whiff of her very specific scent: a combination of fabric softener, Chanel Coco Mademoiselle, and spunkiness. "I formed a swing-dancing team," Megan said confidentially. "We have three couples. I mean, anything goes."

"Swing dancing is a sport?"

"They're trying to get it into the Olympics," Megan said sadly. "It's hard to get respect, but swing dancing takes a lot of athletic ability."

"Hm. Yeah, if curling gets to be in the Olympics, there's pretty much nothing that can't be considered a sport. Even golf," Gaia said.

"Exactly!" For a moment Megan seemed to feel very vindicated. Then she saw the complete lack of expression on Gaia's face and remembered who she was talking to. The freak of the school. "Oh, Gaia. You're being sarcastic again."

Gaia shrugged.

"I wouldn't expect you to understand," Megan complained. "But just look at how excited everyone is." With a sweep of her hand she gestured to the groups of chattering girls and on-a-mission guys crowding the hallway. "You'd do yourself a lot of good if you joined in, Gaia."

"Sure." Gaia hoisted her backpack higher on her shoulder and gave a little nod as she walked off. Wow, Megan had no clue. About anything! *Maybe I should start a dad-finding team,* she thought. *Would that make me more normal in your eyes? But who would I compete against?*

In her rush to get out of the main hallway Gaia took a quick left and felt herself collide with someone. She backed up and muttered an apology, but the someone wouldn't move his lanky frame out of her way. She looked up, about to spit out a withering insult, when she saw that her human obstacle was Jake.

Why did Gaia always call him "snake" in her mind? Despite his friendly words to her the night before, somehow this guy seemed inherently untrustworthy. He was new to the school, and his ridiculously movie-star-level good looks made him a prime target for the FOHs (or FOTs or whatever they were). The most desirable divas in school were working themselves into a group frenzy over him, and he seemed to enjoy the attention—but part of him seemed to stand back, not quite joining in, not quite playing their games.

Of course, Gaia herself was the definition of stand-offish, but she wasn't used to seeing other people hold back like she did. And he did it so subtly, she wasn't even sure she was right about her feelings. She couldn't get a read on him, and that made her suspicious. That plus the fact that he'd challenged her to a karate competition and had very nearly beaten her. That was just not normal. His eyes narrowed as he fixed her with a smile that could only be described as sly.

"Trying to escape the epidemic?" he asked her.

"What epidemic?" she asked warily.

"The school-spirit epidemic," he said. "It's spreading like wildfire. I think they put something in the cafeteria Jell-O."

"That wouldn't spread anything," Gaia informed him. "Nobody in their right mind would eat the cafeteria Jell-O."

"Good point. So you're going to join in, right?"

"Yeah, right." Gaia made a move to pass him, but Jake blocked her way and put a firm hand on her arm. His grip was surprisingly strong.

"I'm serious," he said. "I'm putting together a karate team. We'll beat the pants off of everybody if you and I are on the same team."

"Wow, I so would prefer to see pants remain *on*."

"Don't you want to win? Don't you want to beat these clowns at their own game—literally?"

"You're so goal-oriented," Gaia told him. "I thought intramural week was all for the *fun* of the games."

"Come on," Jake said. "Those were some wild moves you pulled on me. You humiliated me, for chrissake. The least you could do is make it up to me by being on my team."

"Sorry, but I don't need to show off," Gaia told him. "Besides, I've got a new hobby taking up my time."

"What, you're a secret agent?" Jake asked.

Gaia didn't let her surprise show on her face. She

studied Jake carefully secretly, exactly as her father had trained her to do. She took in his body language: His muscular arms, crossed over his chest, said he had something to hide, but he was leaning toward her with his head tilted—which was supposed to indicate that he was friendly and unthreatening. She noticed he was actually just a little too close—was he trying to intimidate her by invading her space? His pupils were dilated, a sure sign he liked what he saw. But his eyes wouldn't quite meet Gaia's, flicking away when she gazed back into them. Damn it. The guy was a walking pile of conflicting information. There had to be something in what her dad told her, some way to read what was behind Jake's words: He seemed to be kidding. She *hoped* he was kidding.

"Secret agent? Right," she said, sliding her own eyes to the side so he wouldn't see how rattled she was. "No, I just really feel that watching paint dry is my true calling," she went on. "It satisfies some deep inner passion."

"That's just how I feel about watching grass grow," Jake retorted, without skipping a beat. "It's so meditative. Almost as good as watching concrete set."

"Ha ha." Gaia almost included a smile in her response. Almost. But Jake seemed happy just to have gotten the "ha ha" out of her.

"Think about it," he said, and walked away.

"Yuh-huh," Gaia said noncommittally, and continued down the hall to her locker. She wondered what was really going on there. Jake wanted something from her. He seemed to be curious—a little too curious. Then again, he could just be flirting with her.

Yeah. Right.

She mulled over the Jake question as she walked down the hall, trying to untangle the strands of information she had from him. She was so distracted, she didn't really notice Ed Fargo walking straight toward her. In fact, she almost said hi to his familiar, loping form.

Then she remembered: The argument. The dismissal. The double-sided promise that they'd keep their distance from each other. Seeing Ed made Gaia feel like hydrogen peroxide had been dumped in a fresh gash in the middle of her gut: It burned and bubbled and ate away at her. Somehow the pain she felt when she saw him was exactly proportional to the closeness they used to have. It was amazing. Best friend had turned to boyfriend and then to total enemy in less time than it took for one of the FOTs to relax a perm. It made Gaia feel sad, sadder than almost anything else in the world, but she wasn't about to let anyone else in on that little secret. Least of all Ed, the guy who was the cause of it.

And here he was. Duh. Of course she was going to have to see him around school. She was going to have to be polite. If not out of respect for their old friendship, then out of the dim hope that the FOTs wouldn't get more fodder for their gossipy bitchfests.

Ed's face didn't betray any emotion. Well, it did, but for him, he was being pretty stoic. Trying to show Gaia a mask of calm. She knew that underneath he was hurting as badly as she was. Stopping about five feet away, his skateboard tucked under his arm, he stood there uncertainly.

"What's up," he said.

"Nothing," she answered, not looking at him.

Gaia's skin felt like it was on fire. The last time she'd seen Ed, he'd been standing on the sidewalk, half drunk, calling her a liar and a cheater and demanding she stay the hell away from him. Her guts turned into a colony of cockroaches, skittering around inside her. She wanted nothing more than to just go back to being friends. But the way he'd spoken to her last night? That wasn't just going to go away. And she had to be honest: She had lied to him. Having Sam show up out of the blue had really knocked her for a loop, and she had been lying to Ed when she'd said she didn't have feelings for Sam anymore. That made her feel horribly guilty. Like maybe Ed was right for wanting to keep his distance. Like maybe she needed to be on her own until she sorted out her unbelievably annoying jumble of emotions.

"So how's Sam," he said, as if he'd been reading her mind and the guilty feelings that were blotched all over it. He was convinced she'd been canoodling with Sam behind his back.

"I don't know. I haven't seen him," she told him, emphasizing the last half of her sentence.

No need to tell him that he'd just tried to kill her. And no need to tell him that before that, Sam Moon's return to the land of the living had made her feel confused. Still, as far as Gaia was concerned, she hadn't *done anything* about her confusion—that was what counted. And Ed was supposed to trust her. And he didn't. Which was why she was pissed.

"So, I'm doing a skateboard clinic as part of intramural week," he said.

"Uh-huh," she murmured. No congratulations, no questions—not even a little bit of teasing about how he was joining in with the school-spirit masses.

This was so WEIRD. Like a new reality show: *When Best Friends Go Bad.* They didn't speak to each other like this. Except they did now. Gaia felt horrible. But this conversation had to end. She needed him to get away from her, fast.

"Yeah. I thought it'd be fun," Ed said. It was a limp, nondescript sentence, and it plopped onto the floor between them and lay there. For Gaia the silence that followed was full of unspoken accusations. *You can't be part of anything, you freak,* he seemed to say. *Like a family. Like a couple. Like anything you desperately want and won't let yourself have.* It stung to hear him say it—stung for the words to be there, sandwiched between the lines in glaring, accusing, ten-foot-high red letters. Without another word Gaia turned back to her locker, hoping he wouldn't see the slight tremble of her chin as she listened to his sneakers squeak down the hall away from her like the turns of a screwdriver driving a rusty screw deep into the soft flesh of her heart.

I wish I didn't have buttons. The same way I don't have fear. I wish nobody could push my buttons the way Ed does, making me feel like everything I do is wrong and useless and mean. I wish that nothing would infuriate me, or make me feel insecure, or rattle my cage.

It's my fault, though. If I hadn't shown Ed where my buttons were, he wouldn't be able to push them.

I thought I was okay, not being close to anyone. I thought I had taught myself not to wish for what I can't have. After my mother died and my father took off, I shut myself off. Personally, I think it was a pretty impressive feat for a kid that young. After a while I didn't know what I was missing.

Well, now I know, don't I? What I'm missing.

Being close to Ed felt like. . . what did it feel like? It wasn't like he was my other half or anything doofy like that. Plato had this whole thing in the *Symposium* about how everyone used to be smushed-together couples with four legs and four arms and their sex organs locked in a constant erotic knot. Then something happened to blow us all apart, and now we spend our whole lives looking for our other halves. I guess some couples feel that way, but not me and Ed.

Still, there was something in the way we were together that was so easy. It felt like *home*. Being with him, being his friend, filled something in me that I didn't know was empty. And then having him become my confidant and my actual boyfriend—that made the connection so much deeper. But the best part was always having him as my friend.

It was a blessing and a curse. The blessing part is what I just said. The closeness. The comfort. The home.

The curse part is that once you've felt that comfort and it's taken away from you, all of a sudden you miss it—even though you never knew you wanted it

before you had it. All these
nerve endings flapping in the
breeze, looking for the tooth
that just fell out.

But there's something bigger—
something worse. Once someone has
been that close to you, he's got
too much on you. He knows how to
hurt you, how to push those goddamn buttons. Hell, he can push
them without even realizing it.

I want to be calm, cool, button-
less. No way in, no way out. Not
even a zipper.

Not fearless, feelingless.
That's a genetic mutation I could
really get behind.

Here is the thing I have to get through my thick, stupid head: The Gaia I fell in love with obviously *does not exist*. Therefore, I do not care that she's gone. Right? WHO CARES? NOT ME. I don't care that she lied, snuck around, maybe even cheated on me with Sam. Since the dependable, honest person I thought she was never existed, technically, I can't miss her. How can you miss a mythical creature? Do I miss unicorns? No. Do I miss the Yeti? No. Do I miss Anna Nicole Smith's dietician? No. And why is that? Because none of those creatures can exist, do exist, will exist. And I don't miss Gaia-my-best-friend because she doesn't exist, either. Now I should be cured.

Except I'm not. The feelings I had for her—the ones that just yesterday were a huge, comfortable blanket around my heart—they just won't get out of me. No matter how much evidence I tally up to the contrary, those feelings want to swim around in my consciousness.

The word *love* keeps floating
around inside my head, like the
afterimage of a flashbulb. Except
in my head the word *love* is purple, and it looks kind of like a
balloon. When I met Gaia for the
first time, I saw that love balloon in my head. It was small
then and just hovered around in
the background as I thought about
calculus, and history, and my
Regents exams. I got to know her
better, and I started to think,
*Maybe I love her. Maybe this word
I've heard about all my life has
a new meaning, maybe it's something I feel for this girl.*

That's when the love balloon
started getting bigger. But the
color of a real balloon gets paler
as it fills with air. The love balloon in my head just became a
richer shade of purple, and when I
thought of Gaia, it got bigger. The
night we spent together, it got
huge. And whatever I was doing in
my day, that purple balloon would
bounce around and make me feel

great, because I knew what it meant
and I felt all this love for this
weird, annoying, funny, crazy girl.
I'd say to myself, like I was trying it out, "Oh, I love Gaia," and
it made me feel so great.

Well, now I don't love Gaia. I
was wrong about her and I was
wrong about feeling that way
about her. But the big purple
love balloon DOES NOT GET THE
MESSAGE. It still bounces around
in my head, but now, instead of
being comforting, it's annoying,
like Barney.

I try to poke it with an imag-
inary needle, but it's made of
some really tough kind of rubber.
I try to make it burst into
flames and hit the ground, like
the *Hindenburg*. Oh, the humanity!
But the damn thing won't deflate
and it won't burst. It's still
hanging out in my head, looming
and bouncing like a permanent
purple storm cloud.

Oh my God. What was that conversation? We're worse than
strangers. It's like we hate each

other. She actually *hates* me. This feels terrible. Cutting off Gaia is like cutting off my own leg—losing it completely, not just having it paralyzed. But she's been lying to me, and I've got to get rid of her now, before I get in even deeper. It'll be better this way in the long run.

The trouble is, how do I make a long run with only one leg?

She should
have been
able to tell
the **plausible**
difference
cover
between a
masked oper-
story
ative and the
president of
the Shakira
fan club.

THANK GOODNESS GAIA HAD OTHER

Yellow Sticky

things to occupy her mind. Her phone finally snapped out of its reverie and went through to Dmitri. Gaia thanked the God of Unpredictable Cell Phone Service and put the phone to her ear.

"Dmitri," she said. "It's Gaia."

"How are you this morning?" he said.

"I'm all right," she lied.

"I thank you again for rescuing me and bringing me back," he said. "My apartment is very comforting to be back in. It is not so much dustier than when I left it."

"Well, good," she said. Was this why he had called? To chat about his one-bedroom in Chinatown?

"I wonder if I can ask for your help," he said, answering her unasked question with his polite segue. "I think I have some information that may be of assistance in finding your father. But I need you to help me get to it. Are you opposed to a little breaking and entering?"

Now this was getting interesting. "Not if it means getting more information about my father," she told him.

"That is good. Your father trained you well."

"I guess. So what's the deal?" she asked him, impatient.

"I don't want to say on the phone," he said. "I've sent you instructions via e-mail. You can go retrieve them."

"Why won't you just tell me?" she seethed.

"Too much to tell," he said. "Too many details. You need to see them and commit them to memory. You should know that this is how things are done in the Organization."

"Yeah, but the Organization should know that e-mail is never secure," she retorted.

"This one is. It's encoded and contains a self-destructing virus. It can only be read once."

"Okay, fine."

"You can check in with me if you have any questions. Otherwise I will expect a visit from you when you've completed the task I've laid out for you."

"Okay." Gaia snapped her phone shut and started to head for the front doors of the school just as the bell rang.

"Gaia Moore," a voice boomed from behind her. She turned to see Vice Principal Lorenz—the grooviest school administrator on the entire East Coast. Lorenz never wore suits, preferring jeans and a sweater, or khakis if he really had to dress up. His thick salt-and-pepper hair had only recently lost its extra ponytail length. Most students liked his get-to-know-you attitude—he acted like the tormented poems of the literary-magazine crew were genius and even thought the cheerleaders were following their bliss. And he liked everyone to call him Bob. Even Gaia thought he seemed cooler than your average schoolhouse bureaucrat—on a normal day. But at this moment he had a distressingly friendly look on his face, like it was time to have a *talk*. And Gaia didn't have time for one of those.

"It looks like you've got somewhere to go," he said.

"No. No, I was just walking. . . past the front door, to my next class," she said. She had to get to a computer and then bust out of school to complete Dmitri's assignment. She wanted to do it now. But Bob Lorenz had a different task in mind.

"I've noticed you've been missing a lot of classes," he said, putting a reassuring hand on Gaia's shoulder. "And even when you're here, you don't really seem *present*. Is something going on?"

Well, let's see. My dad has disappeared, a mysterious old man is sending me on a secret mission, and both my ex-boyfriends are haunting me, in their own special ways.

"No!" Gaia said. "Nothing's going on."

"I know you have an unsettled home life," Bob went on, clamping that hand onto her shoulder and strolling down the hall with her. . . away from the front door. "It must be really tough. If you want to talk about it, you know my door is always open."

Yeah, or I could just watch Dr. Phil, Gaia thought. "I know," she said aloud. "I was actually planning to stop by later this week."

"Well, why don't we just chat now?" he asked, steering her into his office. "I mean, you're here, I'm here. We can talk about all the classes you've missed." He pulled a file out from a stack on top of his desk. It had a yellow sticky on it. Clearly he'd been watching Gaia for a while. . . . She cursed silently. *Should have played my part better,* she grumbled to herself. *I'm setting off alarms left and right.* If the school's administration thought she was some kind of tormented teen in need of intervention, then intervention was what she was going to get—and that meant less freedom to come and go as she pleased. Less freedom to defend herself and find her father.

This was not good.

Every muscle in Gaia's body felt poised for action. Finally there was something she could do about the Mystery of the Missing Parent——and all she had to do was get to a computer to find out what it was. Instead, she was sitting in the vice principal's office, being gently scolded for missing assignments and not being more "proactive in her educational advancement." Ugh.

The intense irony of it was, with one *thunk* of her leg she could have had Vice Principal Bob on the floor and stepped on his unconscious body on the way out the door. But he was a nice guy. And she didn't want to get herself arrested. No, she had to play her part for now; nod and smile as if she understood her shortcomings and really, *really* wanted to better herself. She'd bide her time, make it through this meeting, and check her e-mail in the school library. Whatever was waiting in her in box, it would have to keep for an hour or so.

"STUPID ORGANIZATION," SHE MUTTERED

Constant Skitz

as she waited impatiently for the infuriatingly slow 56-K modem to connect her to the Internet. "Left over from the Cold War. About as updated as Tang or the Fonz. Like this stupid modem," she added, giving the pesky peripheral a whack.

This was a serious breach of security as far as she was concerned. Sending sensitive information over the Internet? Duh. Any twelve-year-old with a Dell could hack into it, encoded or not. Forcing Gaia to read it here, at school? Double duh, ha-doi, and a dah-hicky. This was public property. Maybe the fact that it was teeming with innocent civilians would make a less cynical operative think she was safe here, but Gaia knew her enemies better than that. Her classmates were in as much danger as she was, and whoever was after her—whoever had her father—wasn't going to let a few hundred teenage martyrs stand in his way.

Gaia swallowed hard, the knowledge that she was in constant danger peeking above the surface of her consciousness again. She couldn't live in a state of constant skitz. But she couldn't stop being vigilant, not for even one second. They were after her. Whoever they were. And they'd used something as innocent as a bite of chicken potpie to get her father.

When anything could be a weapon, the world could start looking exceedingly twisted.

The modem finally connected, and she maneuvered through web pages till she got to her e-mail program.

To: gaia13@alloymail.com
From: ruskie@acenet.net

The Worldwide Travel Agency at 53 West 35th Street is a front for the Organization. In there are files pertaining to your father's disappearance. They are labeled *Moorestown* and are enclosed in a brown cardboard accordion folder wrapped with a thick brown string. The label is red. The exact location is not known, but it's most likely in the top drawer of file cabinet A (see map below). Also central to your search is a travel dossier. This is in a yellow file folder in a drawer on the right side of the desk marked *FF*. It is labeled *Places of Interest*. Break in and deliver the files to me today at 5 P.M. at my apartment. Be careful.

Gaia eyed the e-mail with total and complete concentration. She had a photographic memory. The image of the words seared into her frontal lobe as the distractions of the library fell away. There was something meditative about this action: The words became more than black and white on the screen; they took on a life of their own, the shapes of the letters forming patterns that Gaia recognized apart from the meaning of the words themselves. Wow, her brain was freaky sometimes.

A pensive haze settled over her for a moment. There was nothing but the words and the message they brought her. Until a hand clamped over her eyes and the world went dark.

SAM'S POSSESSIONS LAY IN A TANGLED

Stupid Cell Phone

heap on the floor, looking like they'd been ransacked by a couple of angry prison guards. He surveyed the mess with frustration and fury. He couldn't blame anyone but himself for it. He'd been tearing through his own stuff for half an hour, trying to find his cell phone.

He picked up the regular phone and was greeted, yet again, by the incessant whine of an Internet connection. Dmitri was still on-line, and all Sam wanted to do was call Gaia. The guy had been locked up for so long, he hadn't even heard of DSL.

Whatever he was doing, he was doing it at a crawl, and Sam was itching with impatience.

He had an almost physical need to speak to Gaia— it pained him as much as the red scars of the gunshot wounds and operation incision that were the legacy of the time he'd spent in Loki's prison. The last time he'd seen her, she'd been trying like hell to get him out of her apartment while her boyfriend—*her boyfriend!*— read her the riot act in front of her building.

It just killed him. All Sam wanted for Gaia was for her to be happy, and she seemed miserable. Okay, he had to be honest: all he wanted, really, was for Gaia to be happy *with him*. Of course he was jealous that Ed got the title of boyfriend and everything that went with it. *Everything that went with it.* An image of Gaia wrapped in the thin sheets of his dorm-room bed flashed through Sam's brain. He pushed it back into whatever corner it had jumped out of. He was not going to think about that. Gaia had too much going on in her life to deal with Sam's feelings for her. She'd made that much clear. If he'd never been shot, if he'd never disappeared from her life, then things might be different. But they weren't. They were like they were, and he had to keep his distance and give Gaia her space.

But he wanted to call her, anyway. He had to speak to her today. Not to get in her way or push his feelings on her. Just to make sure she was okay. The whole party-packing-fighting-leaving thing the night before had been a situation of such relentless awkwardness, he hadn't been able to relax since.

Forcing himself to take a deep breath and try to relax while he waited for the phone to become available, Sam flopped onto the floor and started doing stretching exercises. The wounds on his back were still raw and painful, but he knew his best chance of healing was to get strong and keep his skin from atrophying into more scar tissue. He could even manage a few push-ups if he really focused. And all through his long imprisonment, there was one image that had helped Sam truly focus: Gaia. He saw her sitting on the edge of his bed, her knees drawn up, the toes of her sneakers pointing toward each other. If he worked out harder, he could even hear her voice.

Very impressive, Sam's inner Gaia said in a flatly sarcastic, teasing voice. *What was that, half a push-up?*

Sam stretched harder, feeling his muscles scream with the effort, but his inner Gaia was right: It wasn't hard enough. This was what he had done the whole time he'd been in that prison. Pictured Gaia to get him through the days. Used the memory of her to force himself to survive. And now he was back in the world with her. Come to think of it, this was probably none too emotionally healthy for him. But he really didn't give a damn: Healthy or not, he needed Gaia to be with him, *really* with him, his girlfriend. They'd had a brief moment of perfect bliss before he'd been captured, and he knew that she could bring him back to that earlier, more innocent, less troubled version of himself. The Sam Moon who was premed at NYU and played a little chess. Who didn't suffer from prison-flashback nightmares. Who wasn't reduced to living in a busted-up apartment in Chinatown where the air smelled like the "fresh" fish store downstairs and the paint on the walls flaked off in lead-filled hunks.

"You picked up the phone again!" Dmitri growled from the next room.

"I need to make some calls," Sam said, stopping his workout and looking up. Sweat poured from his slick skin and his breathing was labored. He was glad to have an excuse to stop, inner Gaia or not. She vanished in a poof from her spot on his bed.

"Use your cell phone," the old man told him, not even turning around from his post at the monitor.

"I told you, I can't find it. I need the phone to at least check my cell's voice mail."

"I am sorry. I must get some things in order."

Sam stood leaning against the doorway, and observed the gnarled fingers tapping away at the keyboard. "I thought you were in that prison for a long time," he said.

"I was, yes," Dmitri said impatiently.

"This iMac is a brand-new model. Did someone buy it for you while you were inside?"

Dmitri turned to him, giving him a baffled, hurt

stare. The old guy had taken a long shower, cut what was left of his thin gray hair, shaved, and served a freedom feast for the two of them the night before, bringing in food from an old-school Romanian restaurant a few blocks away. He was no longer the frail scarecrow that he and Gaia had freed from Loki's prison. His blue eyes had taken on a sharpness, and his muscles seemed to have gained strength overnight. But he was still an old, old man, and one who had just survived a hell of an ordeal.

"Sorry," Sam rushed to say, but Dmitri put up a hand to stop him.

"No, my boy," he said. "I am sorry. I know what it is like to be brutalized the way that you were. I know what it does to you. And I know I am not an ordinary person. All I can tell you is, the years I spent in the Organization left me with many resources. I am not the only one who has used this apartment, though it is my home. Trust me when I say there are certain things you should not know." He shrugged.

Sam nodded and left the room. But the truth was, he really didn't feel any better off here than he had in his cell at the prison. At least there he'd been able to see the bars that held him inside; here, in this apartment, he simply knew that there was danger lurking outside—people trying to recapture him, maybe, or just kill him—and that his life might never get back to normal. Then there was the Gaia question. Which wasn't really a question. It was more a screaming need that wrenched his heart the way his scars wrenched his chest.

He kicked over a milk crate full of his clothes and muttered a stream of curses. He wasn't in school, he had no job (what was he going to put on his resume for his lost semester—"professional prisoner kidnapped by shadowy spylike organization"?), and he didn't even know who he was anymore. *And* he still couldn't find his `stupid cell phone.`

I used to think that there was good and evil and that good would always win out over evil. That's what we're taught to believe, right? That's what always happens on the cop shows on TV. The bad guy might be clever, but *clang clang! Law & Order* will win in the end.

I don't know if I believe that anymore.

I did everything the way I was supposed to. I mean, I wasn't always perfect. I didn't always drive the speed limit, and if the check was wrong, the waitress wasn't going to hear about it from me. But on the whole, I think I tried to do the right thing.

And for most of my life it worked out pretty well.

I don't know, maybe I should have gone to Tufts. Because it was in my second year of NYU that everything started spiraling out of control. I started dating Heather, then she dumped me. I

got seduced by Ella, this older
woman, and then she disappeared,
too. Classes? With all that was
going on, organic chemistry
wasn't exactly foremost in my
mind. And then my roommate got
killed.

And before I could say,
"Prozac, please," my entire exis-
tence was basically wiped from
the earth.

I was shot, sewn together, and
cooped up in a jail cell for no
reason. I got no phone call, no
due process, not even a hint of
what I'd done wrong. . . or
right. I tried to train myself
not to stare up into the sky,
looking for a helicopter full of
good guys who'd rescue me. Not to
look for Superman, or Spiderman,
or even Charlie's Angels.

Sometimes I think about this
guy who lived on my floor in the
dorms. He claimed to be a
nihilist: someone who believes in
nothing. He said no good and
evil, there was no justice or
crime. I thought about him a lot

when I was locked up. I thought, *If I can be like that, if I can believe there's no reason or pattern in the world, then I'll stop believing there's hope, I'll stop hoping for release.* Because it was the hope that was killing me.

But I never managed to believe in nothing. And you know what? Neither did the guy on my floor. Because when he got a phone call telling him his father was dead, I saw him cross himself. Even the nihilist believed, just for a moment, when things got bad enough. And I did, too. I believed I'd get out of there.

And then I did. Okay, so it wasn't an action hero who rescued me, it was Gaia and Dmitri. But the thing I had hoped for? It came true. That should tell me that there is good in the world, right? And that good triumphs over evil, setting the innocent free and bringing justice in its wake?

But the big day of my rescue was just like any other day. The

sun set, and it rose the next
day, and I still didn't have any
answers about why this had happened to me. And I'm not any more
free than I was behind bars. And
worst of all, the bad guys are
still out there.

So what does that mean,
Bosley?

All I know is, the last time I
felt good, the last time the
world made sense, I was with
Gaia. Wrapped in my sheets and
feeling her strong body next to
mine, watching her let go of all
that tough-bitch bullshit and
just melt into my arms. I want to
feel that way again.

Can being with her bring me
back to that place? I don't know.
But nothing else seems to be
working. I guess I'd really like
to find out. I guess I need to
see for myself if Gaia can bring
the world back into focus for me.

GAIA WHIPPED HER ARMS BEHIND

Bigger Fish

her and grabbed whoever had their hands clamped over her eyes. With one brisk movement she had her attacker slammed on a library table, faceup, with her forearm against their throat, ready to rip out their. . .

It was Megan.

Her hazel eyes were wide with surprise, and she was making a faint choking noise. Gaia let go of her throat and stood up, snapping off the monitor behind her with her other hand.

"Huccch," Megan said, rubbing her throat and giving Gaia a confused and angry stare. She sat up on the table. "You're such a freak. What the hell is wrong with you?"

"Why did you attack me?" Gaia asked flatly. The truth was, she felt like a total idiot—she should have been able to tell the difference between a masked operative and the president of the Shakira fan club, for chrissake. And that made her even more aggressively angry.

"I was just trying to goof around with you," Megan snapped, her hand still fluttering protectively around her throat. "Jesus. You were so wrapped up in the computer, I thought it was funny. I was just going to say '*guess who*.'"

"You can't sneak up on people like that," Gaia told her.

"Oh, please. Would you give it up already?" Megan

seemed exasperated. "When are you going to learn that you're not fooling anybody?"

"What the hell is that supposed to mean?"

"I mean, nobody buys your 'I'm so mysterious, try to figure me out' act. Like you're the tormented star of some movie of the week. Everybody just thinks you're pathetic. Your psycho party-pooper routine last night went a long way toward convincing everyone you've got serious emotional issues. And when I tell them you attacked me just to increase the faux mystique, your stock'll take even more of a nosedive."

"Well, thank you so much for the insight," Gaia said. "It's really comforting to know I'm being psycho-analyzed behind my back by someone who thinks swing dancing is a sport."

Gaia didn't know whether to be relieved or insulted. Okay, she was both. Relieved that she *was* fooling everybody. And insulted that they thought she was a stereotypical tortured teen. Well, at least she had a plausible cover story.

"Why don't you do yourself a favor and take some advice," Megan said. "Stop assuming I'm an idiot just because I'm popular. And join a team—*any* team— before you become one of those lonely old people with twenty cats whose only close personal relationship is with a phone psychic."

"Yes, I'm sure spending time with people who share my intense interest in bowling will really draw me out of my shell and provide me with the life skills I need," Gaia snapped.

"Suit yourself," Megan told her. "You know, frankly, I don't give a crap what you do. I just felt sorry for you. When you're a lonely thirty-year-old writing memoirs about how miserable your younger days were, like Janeane Garofolo or Margaret Cho, don't you dare say nobody ever tried to get through to you." She stalked off.

Gaia stared after her. *Well, well, well,* she thought. *Little Megan was on a mission to do some good works. I hope she gets a gold star for trying.*

Whatever. Gaia had bigger fish to fry. She still had the information in her head, which was good, because when she turned the monitor back on, she could see that the message had already self-destructed. With a few flicks of the mouse she emptied the computer's cache, just to be on the safe side. The fun was over. Now she had to get to Midtown—fast.

Ready to Spring

"I SWEAR, ONE OF THESE DAYS WE'RE going to see Gaia on the cover of the *New York Post*, being led into a squad car in handcuffs," Megan complained to Tatiana five minutes later. "No offense, but I don't know how you can be friends with her. Let alone Heather. She's totally nutso."

"It is not easy," Tatiana agreed, checking her lipstick in her locker mirror. Her lilting Russian accent was still apparent, but her English improved by the day, and as it did, her shyness seemed to melt away. So much so that her position as nouvelle Heather seemed completely natural. "She can be a most unusual roommate," she added. "Sometimes I expect to see her sleeping upside down, like a bat. Has she done something to you today?"

"Well, yeah. I just went up to her in the library and tried to be friendly—for your sake, I guess," Megan answered. "But she was so wrapped up in her geekoid computer world that she flipped out the minute I touched her. I mean, it was so totally over the top, I could have had her arrested for assault. She must be involved in one of those on-line role-playing games. She probably forgot about reality for a second and thought she was really Astrella, Queen of the Dark Demons." She gave an evil titter. "Do you think she dresses up like an elfin waif on the weekend and meets up with Renaissance Faire weirdos for some naughty jousting?"

Megan let out a loud guffaw at the thought of Gaia in a green doublet and hose, but Tatiana just turned to her with a blank expression on her face.

"What was she doing on the computer? Did you see what was on the screen?"

"No. It was probably naked pictures of the cast of *Buffy the Vampire Slayer*."

"Was it e-mails? Did you see what any of them said?" Tatiana asked in a curiously intense voice.

"I don't know, maybe. It did look like she was reading e-mails, and she was totally focused, like they were full of secrets or something."

"Are you sure you didn't see what any of them said?"

Megan looked at Tatiana. "Jeez, no, Tat. I mean, come on, who cares, right?" She gave a little laugh, then looked expectantly at Tatiana, who fixed her eyes on her new friend for a moment longer, then gave in and laughed, too.

"I just thought it would be such good gossip if you saw something." She shrugged. "I never can figure out what Gaia is up to. I thought you might have seen what the big secret was."

"The big secret is there is no big secret," Megan said decisively. "Are you hung over? I'm hung over huge, and I think I'm going to run to Starbucks between classes. You want to come?"

Tatiana turned away and seemed to be staring into the black recess of her locker. Megan didn't notice that Tatiana's spine was curiously tense, that she was wound as tight as a coil ready to spring.

"No, thank you." Tatiana's voice drifted over her shoulder. "I just remembered, there is a phone call I must make."

Tatiana closed her locker and stepped toward one of the wide windows that would afford her cell phone the best reception. She flicked it open, murmuring into it in serious Russian tones that seemed out of place in the teeming high school hallway. If Megan had noticed, she might have found it odd. But she didn't notice. No one did. And after a little while Tatiana snapped her phone closed. Then she pulled a second cell phone out of her bag, checking closely to see if any messages had popped up on its small screen. Then she put both phones away and strolled down the hall as if she didn't have a care in the world.

The jangling

bells of the

antitruant

alarm

exploded in **rules**

her ears.

ED STRODE PAST THE LIBRARY, AND

for the second time that day he caught the familiar sight of Gaia's long, straight blond hair. His reflex reaction was to rap on the window and say hi, but he stopped himself just in the nick of time.

Off-limits

When was he going to get it through his thick head—or his thick heart? `Gaia: off-limits.` He knew it intellectually, but the rest of him—every bit of him from the neck down, including the heart and various other regions—hadn't yet gotten the news.

Without realizing it, Ed leaned his head against the window of the library and sighed.

"Oh, my goodness, who is sad today? Perhaps you are hung over like Megan. Would you like to get some coffee?"

The musical Russian accent, the friendly voice—he hated to admit how good it felt to see Tatiana coming up to him.

"Hey!" he said. "How are you doing? You were pretty wrecked last night."

"Oof!" Tatiana waved a hand in the air. "I have almost no memory of the party. My apartment is such a mess, I have to have someone help me clean. I hope you had a fun time?"

Ed shrugged. Actually, the party had been a night-mare: obnoxious girls, too much Sam Adams, guys who thought "woo!" was a conversation aid, and of course his horrible confrontation with Gaia after he'd found her in a love knot with Sam. He hoped Tatiana really didn't remember much. Jeez, she'd been so drunk, she'd come on to him, and he'd been so drunk, he'd almost let her. But as he studied her face, there didn't seem to be any awkwardness in her gaze.

"I had a fine time," he said. "I don't remember much, either."

There. They were both off the awkwardness hook, using the age-old beer-amnesia excuse. Gosh, it was handy. Now all the awkwardness he felt was the regular old I-don't-know-you-well-enough kind. Which was kind of okay, actually. Interesting. Possibly even a little exciting.

"Are you going to do an intramural?" Tatiana asked him.

"Yeah, a skateboarding clinic," he told her.

"Oh, that is so perfect for you!" Tatiana cried, slapping him on the arm. "And after you couldn't do it for so long, now you'll be teaching it to the younger students—Ed, that is really cool."

Now, see? How hard is it to just be happy and supportive? Is Gaia just lacking this skill altogether? This is how friends are supposed to act together.

"I'm actually pretty psyched," Ed admitted. He shifted his feet, feeling self-conscious, not sure if he needed to explain. "I never thought I'd be teaching anything, but when they asked me, I was just like, what

49

the hell. I'm sure they'll regret ever considering such a thing, especially when I take a bunch of freshmen into the abandoned pool in Williamsburg and we all get arrested."

"Ed, don't be silly. They wouldn't have asked you if they didn't think you could do it. You'll be a great teacher."

The way that Tatiana looked at Ed with her big blue eyes made him feel ten feet tall. Never mind that the eyes he'd prefer to see gazing at him were ice blue and belonged to Gaia. Never mind that Tatiana didn't hold quite the same fascination for him—that she was sweet and funny but didn't have quite the same spark as Gaia. Gaia had taken herself out of Ed's circle of friends. And Tatiana clearly wanted to be in that circle. Could you blame a guy for feeling good about that? It was just the antidote Ed needed.

"Yeah, well. So what about you? Starting a ski team or something?"

"I'm going to do something, but I'm not sure what," she said. "Perhaps running track or something boring like that."

"That's not boring," Ed told her. "And it comes in handy when you're running late to catch a bus."

"Now, you see, that is good common sense," Tatiana told him. "I knew I would learn good life skills in your American high school."

The banter between them was easygoing and fun,

good-natured and friendly. After a while the heart-break Ed was feeling receded from the front of his consciousness. Without realizing it, some of the lead in his chest leaked out, just a little. Tatiana had some kind of effect on him. Enough to make him stop seeing Gaia everywhere he looked and start having fun again. For a moment. For a little while.

And it felt—if not all better, halfway normal. For Ed, that was the hugest relief of all.

GAIA'S NEXT CLASS WAS AP ENGLISH.

Low-Rent Drug Deal

The class was about halfway through a long discussion of *Hamlet*; today they were going to watch scenes from the movie versions starring Ethan Hawke, Kenneth Branagh, and Mel Gibson and compare them to one another. Literature via Hollywood.

Gaia had read *Hamlet* in sixth grade. She really didn't care what Hollywood had done with it. And quite frankly, the story of a guy whose father was d-e-a-d dead and whose son was haunted by the need to avenge him was completely not what Gaia needed—or wanted—to think about.

It shouldn't bother me, she told herself. *Because my dad is not dead. He's just missing.*

Right. And she was the one who had to find him. Pronto.

Before the between-class bell could ring a second time, Gaia was clear of any part of the school where she might be spotted by someone other than a stray mouse. Contrary to what Vice Principal Bob thought, she had done a lot of studying in high school. But the knowledge she'd squirreled away had nothing to do with *The Red Badge of Courage* or pi-*r*-squared—stuff she'd mastered years before and didn't feel the need to show off about. The most useful information she had acquired in recent months had more to do with blueprints—as in, the layout of her school, from top to bottom, complete with emergency escape routes for times just such as this.

She admired the purpose of the antitruant rules that were supposed to keep her here. But they were getting in the way.

Most of the doors to the basement were wired with alarms, but Gaia had noticed that the school janitors were easily annoyed—particularly by oversensitive bells that went off accidentally when they were just trying to clean up a chem lab spill. At least half of the doors were disabled, a fact she'd noticed when a gang of ersatz bad-kid freshmen had gone through a phase of daring each other to set off the alarms on purpose.

It had kept not working. Gaia had noted the location of the dead doors for future reference.

That knowledge came in handy now. She made her way to a corner of the school near the sidewalk and hit the red lever of the door smack in the middle of the word *warning*. Seconds later Gaia Moore vanished from the smooth tiled hallways of her high school and into the dusty dank basement below.

She heard the metal stairs clank under her feet as she made her way down into the gloom. It was so gross down here, even the most hot-blooded adolescents wouldn't want to use it as a make-out spot. The heater and water boiler were ancient and had sprung quite a few leaks over the years, creating the kind of moldy environment that silverfish and millipedes found irresistible.

Gaia was sure nobody would be down here. Too sure.

"Who's that?" she heard a voice say. She froze, cursing herself for not having tiptoed down the metal stairs. The silence around her was broken only by the throbbing hum of the boiler. As her eyes adjusted to the gloom, she looked out into the open space of the basement and saw three nervous-looking students peering around, a triptych of paranoid self-preservation. One of them—a kid Gaia recognized as a self-styled wanna-be wise guy—was holding out a couple of mini-baggies of what looked to be weed. The other kids were holding money. This was nothing more than a `low-rent drug deal`, and it was none of her business.

But before she could melt back into the shadows, something conked her on the head from behind. Her relief turned to fury as she hit the ground, knocked off balance by the sneak attack.

"What the—"

Gaia saw an overgrown hulk standing over her with a lead pipe still held over his shoulder like a softball bat.

"What the hell are you doing down here?" he demanded.

Gaia saw the two buyers race up the stairs and disappear through the door back into the school, a momentary sliver of light announcing their departure. The back of her head burned, and she could hear a loud ringing in her ears. But the dizziness retreated almost immediately. The blow to her melon might have trounced a normal kid, but Gaia was anything but normal.

"Crap, they took their money with them," the dealer groaned. As he turned toward her, Gaia got a good look at him. His mussy hair was in dire need of a bottle of Pantene, and he wore a denim jacket emblazoned with Megadeth patches over a hooded sweatshirt. Worst of all, his upper lip held a smudge of peach fuzz that she was sure he intended to pass off as a mustache. "Who messed up my deal? Brick, man, what do I keep you around for?"

Brick just glared down at Gaia. His bulk was the

most noticeable thing about him: Some pituitary mis-
fire had given him the body of a wrestler, and his
shaved head only served to enhance the impression
that he had absolutely no neck whatsoever. "She
came out of nowhere, Skelzo," he complained. "I
didn't see her till she was practically on top of you."

Skelzo walked over and glared at Gaia, who was
patiently waiting for these two nonentities to get tired
of talking so she could get out of there.

"Girlfriend, you wandered into the wrong part of
school," he told her.

"Oh, no, I'm petrified," she said. "Can I leave now
if I promise never to come back?"

"You'll run straight to the principal's office," he
scoffed.

"I won't, I swear." Gaia was finding it increasingly
difficult to play the part of terrified teen, however
half-assed her attempt already was. "I'll get in as much
trouble as you if anyone finds out I was down here,"
she pointed out. "Just let me go and I promise I'll forget anything ever happened."

"Oh, you'll forget, all right." Skelzo's scraggly
mouth twisted into a grin. "You'll forget because I'll
make you forget."

She rolled her eyes. "What does that even mean?"
she asked.

"What?"

"I mean, *you'll make me forget?* What, did you read

that in a comic book and think it would sound good? It doesn't even make sense as a threat."

"Look, bitch, you better—"

"No, you bogus tool, *you'd* better." Gaia kicked directly up and into Skelzo's crotch, lifting him into the air with the force of her blow. He gave a kitten-like mew of pain as he arced backward, and when he hit the ground, he curled into a ball without another sound.

Brick was faster on his feet than Gaia had expected, and he brought the lead pipe down toward her. She rolled to get out of his way, but the pipe still glanced off her shoulder, creating a searing white-hot flash of pain instantly.

"Ow," she complained, rolling into a crouch and eyeballing her opposition. "Brick, why don't you just run? I promise you'll be better off."

Brick only stared at her, crouching slightly as he poised to swing at her again the second she moved. He was a good fighter, she noted. Or he could be if he trained. This self-taught tough guy was about to find out that brawn wasn't the only thing he needed to beat some ass.

"I really don't have time for this," she complained. Then she shot forward, grabbing him around the waist and pushing him backward onto the floor. Landing on top of his massive frame, she straddled his chest and grabbed both sides of his head, bringing it down to smack against the cold concrete. She heard an "uggh," but when she leapt to her feet, the stupid doofus still wanted to come after her. Stealing a glance at Skelzo, she saw he was puking up his guts and clutching his stomach; at least she didn't have to worry about him. She stopped Brick with a foot to the chest, then moved her foot six inches higher to smack him back down with another shot to the forehead.

Blood splattered where his scalp scraped the concrete. "Shit," Gaia muttered. These were just a couple of kids in her way, not a true threat, and she didn't want to do real damage to them. "You total idiot, why didn't you just back off before I hurt you?" she asked.

Leaving the Moron Twins flat on the floor, Gaia turned toward the trapdoor to the sidewalk that would lead her to freedom. Then she heard a groan. She turned back to look and saw more blood leaking out from Brick's head wound.

Forget him, she told herself. *You have a job to do.*

But some sneaky little sliver of conscience yanked her mind back into the basement. These weren't Loki's henchmen. They were a couple of stupid pot-dealing teenagers. And if she left them bleeding in the basement, they might not be found for hours—even days.

She gave a hefty sigh and ran across the basement, leaping up the metal steps of another set of stairs toward a door that would trip the alarm. She leapt up and snapped her foot out, hitting the door with percussive force and shoving the door open with whatever was the direct opposite of delicacy. It slammed open with a clang, and the jangling bells of the alarm exploded in her ears.

It would only be a matter of moments before someone came in the open door. She raced back across to the trapdoor set into the ceiling under the sidewalk, throwing herself against it with the strength of a bucking horse. It held fast. She cursed, then threw herself against it again. Obviously it was padlocked from the outside. Gaia looked around wildly, feeling her adrenaline rise as the alarm bells continued to jangle. She wasn't worried about being punished. She was worried about how this would slow her down. And getting slowed down was not an option.

Her eyes rested on a red fireman's ax. Never mind that a high school was a horrible place to leave a lethal weapon; she was glad to see it. Angling it between the door and its frame, she placed the sharp edge against the crack and whacked it. Once, twice. . . and on the third hit she felt the metal hinge snap and give above her hands. She pushed the door open and leapt up, swinging her legs and pushing her arms down so she could reach the sidewalk. She rolled away from the gaping door and came face-to-face with Karl, the hot dog vendor who tortured the students with his heaven-scented Sabrett cart.

"Now, I know you're not supposed to be out here," he said, giving an amused shake of his head.

"I'm not planning on sticking around," she told him.

"Hey, you want to cut school, go right ahead," he said. Without another word Gaia stood, kicked the door closed, and raced uptown.

"But you oughta go back," Karl yelled after her. "Unless you wanna be selling wieners for a living when you're my age!"

By the time anyone noticed she was gone, Gaia was halfway to Midtown on the 1 train.

Tatiana —

What is up? I just had a mocha latte and I am buzzing from a sugar high and caffeine, but guess what? I am still hung over! I am chugging vitamin water to escape this hell. If you have any Motrin, please chuck it my way.

DWI = drunk woman intoxicated.

So by the way, I saw you talking to Ed! <u>What is going on there, girlfriend?</u> It looks like you two are already BFGF. You've got more chemistry than seventh period HA HA! You'd better watch out for the psycho beast known as G. M.! Make sure she's done with that toy b/f you play with it! Otherwise you might find yourself picking teeth out of your ass <u>or worse</u>!!! DSIDWIf (don't say I didn't warn you).

Seriously, I think u 2 (ohmigod! My favorite band!) would be the cutest couple. You should jump on that. When Heather was with him, she said he had a way with his tongue — I mean when they were kissing!!! I hope Heather is OK. I keep meaning to call her, but I'm being such a flake about it. I want to tell her about the benefit, but first I want to find out how much $$$ we made. Thanks to you and your connections, girlfriend! You are the best!

Uh-oh I can see Mrs. Hochman giving me the evil eye. If she busts me I'll get detention for sure TTYL!

                — Megan

GAIA HAD NEVER BEEN TO CALCUTTA,

Chubby Airplane

but she had heard about the wall-to-wall throngs on the sidewalks, the makeshift bazaars where people sold fruit, the crowds that slowed foot traffic to a crawl. Midtown Manhattan on a weekday—especially here, in the part of town called the Garment District—had to be a lot like it, she thought. There were just so many people going to their jobs, from their jobs, delivering things from one job to another. Entire racks of clothes bumped down the sidewalk, bright colors standing out against the gray and grayer buildings, sleeves billowing out as if they were being strutted down a catwalk instead of being wheeled by poverty-income dudes who barely noticed the fabulousness they transported. If she'd wanted to, she could have bought batteries (*Energizer!*) or a watch (*Bolex!*) or pirated DVDs of the top ten movies playing in the theaters that week. Or she could have ducked into Macy's and joined the tourists going up and down the building's ancient wooden escalators to buy Charter Club ties and sweaters. Or she could've gotten on a train bound for suburban New Jersey heading out of Penn Station. But she had no interest in any of this. She was headed for the travel agency.

The avenues in this part of the city seemed impossibly long, probably because they were sandwiched between tall, looming buildings that barely left a wedge of street between them. In some places the sunshine barely hit the pavement; the sunniest day could feel like an overcast mess if you never walked west. The address she was looking for was here, right in the middle of the block, in a storefront that seemed almost abandoned among the bustling wholesale clothing stores and office buildings whose revolving doors never stopped turning.

The travel agency's storefront was grimy, and the only decoration was a once cheerful cardboard sign in the shape of a `chubby airplane` announcing new low fares to Yugoslavia. It took a few moments for Gaia to even find the door, which gave a desultory jingle when she opened it. Inside, the gloom was interrupted only by the dust that seemed to have collected in every corner. The dropped ceiling featured broken asbestos tiles and fluorescent tube lights, most of which were either completely dim or flickering faintly. Four industrial-size desks sat facing the center of the room, like a cloverleaf, and Gaia noted that the file cabinets were exactly where they were supposed to be according to Dmitri's e-mail. She was able to match the room around her to the map in her head perfectly.

Only one of the desks was occupied, by a woman who seemed to be the exact color of the grayish linoleum. "Can I help you?" she asked uncertainly, as if a customer were a rare bird she hadn't sighted in several years.

"Yeah, I go to NYU, and I intern down the street," Gaia told her, using her well-crafted cover story. "I was on my way to work when I noticed you're a travel agency. I wanted to know if you had any ideas for where I could go on my winter break."

"Oh. . . I don't know," the woman said, staring down at the brochures piled on her desk as if they would crumble to dust if she tried to open them. "We mostly do corporate travel."

"But look right here!" Gaia pressed a finger onto the top brochure. "It says 'student travel specials.' Those look good—can I find out more about them?"

"Oh," the woman said. "I forgot about that. Well, you can look through it if you want. But you know, I'm not sure if we can help you. I'm not used to booking individual trips."

"I have to go home, anyway, and check out the choices with my suite mates," Gaia told her. "Will you be open late tonight?"

"We stay open till seven," she said.

The phone on her desk gave a bleating ring, and the woman stared at it in alarm.

"Excuse me," she said to Gaia, who was pretending to leaf through the brochure as she took in the rest of the office.

"Yes. Yes. No, not really. Yes. No. Okay," she said into the phone. "Not now. I am! Okay. Yes. Sure." Then she hung up and peered at Gaia.

"I'm sorry, I have to close up the shop right now," the woman told Gaia.

"I thought you said you were open till seven!" Gaia said in her best complainy-student voice. Inside, she was beaming: Dmitri was right. This place was such a front, it might as well have NOT A TRAVEL AGENCY, KEEP WALKING emblazoned on its sign outside.

"Normally we are, but that was my boss, and he said he wants the place closed up for some reason."

"Man, this sucks," Gaia said, still in her college-girl persona. "How am I going to book my trip?"

"Try Orbitz," the woman told her.

Gaia gave an exasperated sigh and left the agency. Just before she exited the door, she looked back: The woman, who just moments before had been so distracted she couldn't even focus on Gaia's request was suddenly going through the contents of her desk with well-organized speed. The soft bafflement of her features had been replaced with a razor-sharp grimace of concentration. `Oh, man, was this place a front!` In essence, a file bank for the Organization. Gaia couldn't wait to come back. All she had to do was wait for this weird chick to clear out and the place was all hers. Better than a playground. And educational, too.

In the meantime Gaia was glad to take a breather from the place. Something about it gave her the willies. The travel posters were all too enthusiastic— and about places where nobody in their right mind would really go on vacation. Clearly they had been fashioned by people with nothing but disdain for the common sense of the average customer. It was as if the Organization were subtly making fun of every unsuspecting civilian who walked through the door. Like they were playing games with people's lives and it was all the more fun for them that those people didn't know about it.

She couldn't wait to rip these jackasses off.

Are you tired of traveling to the same well-worn destinations?

Experience the land of bleak mountains and turbulent rivers. Unite with nature in a sparsely populated region nearly untouched by civilized man. Come face-to-face with the Snow Man—and barely live to tell the tale! Come to beautiful Siberia!

See your representative now.
It may be the last trip you ever want to take!

To: shred@alloymail.com
From: gaia13@alloymail.com
Re: Hope you are OK

I feel really bad about how things ended
between us and I just wanted to say I hope we can
be friends at some point. I wish I could explain
why I snuck around and what was going on. But I
can't because slkdfjsghsoioiffdkslf THIS SOUNDS
SO STUPID.

<DELETED>

To: shred@alloymail.com
From: gaia13@alloymail.com
Re: Wish things had been different

I hate the way things ended between us, but it
just has to be this way for now. I have some
crazy stuff going on and I'm just not going to be
a good girlfriend, and it's not fair to you. I
just wish you had trusted me more. Not that I
really gave you much reason to. OH, SCREW THIS.

<DELETED>

To: shred@alloymail.com
From: gaia13@alloymail.com
Re: Hi

You were my best friend and I'll never forget
that. Thank you for the time we spent together.
It really was the best.

<STORED ON HARD DRIVE—UNSENT>

The pungent
odor of
gasoline
hit her
nostrils
just as she
realized
what was
happening.

the

flame

IT TOOK EXACTLY TWENTY MINUTES

for Gaia to walk across the street, order one of the best falafels she'd ever had, and chew it slowly at a window table. The whole time, she kept her eyes on the travel-agency-slash-Organization-front. The woman from the desk left almost immediately, but Gaia knew not to count on that. She wanted to make sure the woman didn't come back—either to catch her or to get something she'd forgotten. But as Gaia wadded up the aluminum foil and wiped the last of the tahini sauce from the corners of her lips, the coast seemed as clear as it was going to get. It was time to make her move.

The first thing she noticed when she walked into the building next door was that the elevator shaft connected the two buildings. That was good news: If she could get in there, she'd have a strong chance of breaking through to the travel agency without alerting anyone on the street.

The trouble was, she had to get into that elevator shaft.

"Can I help you?" a voice came from behind her. Gaia turned to see a tall, hefty guy in coveralls. Earl, his name tag read in embroidered script. Standing between her and the elevator.

"Is this where Casa del Carpets is?" she asked, putting a hand on her hip and letting Earl get a good long look at her. She was wearing a tank top—it was almost guaranteed Earl wasn't going to remember her face.

"No, it's not," he said to her chest. "Casa del Carpets is down the street."

"Ohmigod, sorry to bother you. Thanks," Gaia said, and left the building.

Oh, great. That was one of the dumbest moves she'd ever made. Walked right into a security guard, or elevator operator, or whatever he was. She had to get past that guy and into the elevator—and there was no guaranteeing she'd get through the shaft even if she did get in there. Damn it, Gaia could *feel* time slipping away.

As if on cue, a huge dump truck, trundling down the street, stopped a few feet away. The driver got out and ran into a deli. Gaia could see him directing the guy behind the counter to pour him some coffee. This was her shot, and she took it.

In a flash she was up in the cab of the truck, faced with the dashboard. Mostly it looked like the usual car controls, but below the stereo, on the floor, there was a huge black box with an extra set of buttons. If she could just figure out which one. . .

CLANG!

That was it! The back of the truck began rising, lifted by the huge hydraulic cylinders that unfolded from its belly. Gaia pulled back on the lever that made it rise faster. If she was right about her calculations, the pile of garbage in the dump bed was too heavy to stand for much of a—

THUD!

Gaia felt the truck pitch backward as its dump bed hit the asphalt behind it, pulling the front wheels right off the ground. She gave a nervous laugh: It felt like an earthquake, the way the concrete buckled under the truck, and the huge load of ash created a choking cloud that gave Gaia just the cover she needed. She whisked out of the passenger door of the truck before the driver could get out of the deli and was safely in a crowd on the sidewalk by the time he ran up to the cab of his truck, frantically tugged at the controls, and waved his arms, as though that were going to undo what Gaia had done. The truck was a mess and would be completely unmovable until all the ash was cleared away. More important, everyone on the street was awestruck by the colossal mess.

Including Earl.

With the elevator guy gaping openmouthed and watching as police cars sped onto the scene, Gaia had the opening she needed. She slipped into the building, stepped into the old-school elevator, and yanked a huge metal lever back so that the doors closed.

"Hmmm," she said. The walls of the elevator enclosed her, but she wasn't moving. A huge old crank stood to her right. She turned it and the elevator lurched upward. She rode it too fast up two floors, then brought it gently down so that she was between one and two. Then she yanked open the doors again, exposing the dank shaft in all its concrete-and-metal glory.

Layers and layers of filth, going back half a century or so, caked the walls. The only things that looked well used were the gears and cables, slick with oil, that kept the thing in motion. Gaia peered down into the shaft. She thought she could shimmy through the narrow hole into the open area below her. But once down there, she had to hope there was some way out. Because if the elevator went into motion, she'd be crushed like a bloody, bony pancake.

Still, it was her best option. She thought she saw a ventilation shaft opening down there. There was only one way to find out if she was right: She squeezed her legs into the narrow opening between the door of the elevator and the wall of the shaft, then shifted her hips so they hitched through the tiny space.

"Ow," she muttered, feeling the uneven edge of the elevator's lip scrape the button of her jeans. Then the cold metal grated against her chest, and for an awful moment she thought the life was being squeezed out of her as her lungs fought for air. Then she was through, hanging in the dim light of the elevator shaft, peering across to see if she was right about the way through to the other building—the one where the travel agency was.

There it was. A ventilation hole. She had to make it across the bottom of the elevator somehow. The ventilation system went along the ceiling of the room below, and if she plopped to the ground, she'd have a hell of a time getting back up.

She hoped the grease of the cables hadn't pervaded the metal bottom of the elevator car. It hadn't—but the grime was so thick, it was almost as slippery. She had one chance to get across, and it hinged on one metal pipe attached to the elevator. She reached out and grabbed for the pipe.

The dust made her hand slip right off. Her hand slid out into space, and she felt her left shoulder socket wrench with the effort of keeping her from falling.

"Huuugh," she gasped, more from the pain and surprise than from any real concern that she'd fall. She had this under control. She just had to make it happen. And fast.

"Hello? What the hell is going on in here?"

Uh-oh. Really fast. Earl was back on the scene, and if he started up that elevator. . .

Gaia wiped the thick layer of dust off her hand and onto her jeans and reached for the pipe again. Not a great grip, but it was all she had, and as she swung across the bottom of the elevator, she felt herself slipping slightly.

"Easy," she told herself. No need to grab too hard.

Gaia swung her legs across and tested the metal

door of the ventilation hole. It was as old as the building—older than her father, probably—and it didn't want to give.

Gaia heard Earl come out of the landing on the second floor. He'd obviously taken the stairs up and was looking down into the empty elevator.

"Hello? Damn kids! Who's down there?"

She heard him swear a blue streak as he kicked at the elevator. It shuddered above her, making her already tenuous grasp feel even less secure.

"Damn it," she hissed.

"What? Is somebody down there?"

This was getting ridiculous. Gaia tightened her grip on the pipe. She heard Earl's feet hit the floor of the elevator just above her, and it shuddered again. Earl was not light. The elevator shifted at least two inches lower and began to rock. She had to get into that ventilation crawl space—*now*.

Gaia lifted her legs and kicked. Once. Twice. Three times. And then—"Jaah!" she yelled, `feeling the metal door give as she gave it one last kick.` The elevator shuddered again as she heard the machinery start up, high above her. With no time to waste she kicked the door out of the way and shoved her legs into the dark, musty tube. She pulled herself all the way in just as the elevator dropped past. A hunk of her hair got yanked along with it, and she grabbed at it, forcing it to break rather than pull her along its deadly track. Then she just breathed, feeling her racing heart, pumped full of adrenaline, try to return to normal.

She assessed her surroundings. She could feel that she had just inches of steel through which she had to shimmy backward to reach anything close to the travel agency. Behind her she could hear the alarmed skittering steps of water bugs and maybe even a rat or two. Gross. Gross, but not life-threatening. She began her slow journey backward. "I must look really pretty right now," she said to herself, feeling dust coat her skin as she pulled herself through it. But once she got started, she found herself making good progress— below her, through the slatted openings, she could see a hallway, and then, a few minutes later, the dim interior of the travel agency.

Bingo.

She held her face close to the thin opening, trying to see what was on the various desks below her. Ugh, it was no use. She jimmied her fingers under the edge of the covering and yanked it up. The place was empty; she didn't care about the noise. She remembered how dank the place had smelled when she'd walked in before—funny how after ten minutes in an elevator shaft, it smelled as fresh as a springtime meadow.

Now she could see. But she needed to be down there, going through the desks, finding the files that Dmitri needed.

Dropping to the floor, Gaia wasted no time. The gate covering the front window was down, so she had to work in near darkness. She had two things to find: the travel folder, which had an exact location, and the file on her father, which had only an approximate location. She knew that no matter what her emotional priorities were, she had to look for the one she was assured of finding first. She went to desk FF and yanked open the drawers on the right side until she found a yellow file folder labeled *Places of Interest*.

Seeing that folder fired her impatience. Adrenaline shot through her veins, and some unholy combination of joy and vindication filled her heart—she had the right place; the directions were correct. Now all she had to do was find the Moorestown folder and she'd be on her way out.

She shoved the yellow folder down the back of her pants for safekeeping and turned to file cabinet A. A quick search of the drawers revealed a lot of cardboard accordion folders wrapped with thick brown string— but none of them had a red label marked with any- thing akin to *Moore, Moorestown,* or *Moore*—anything.

Okay. No problem. Gaia set her jaw and turned to the next file cabinet, moving systematically through the drawers in search of the Tom Moore folder. Then she moved to the next one. With each failure and each opening of a new drawer, her movements became slightly more agitated. In her experience, if something wasn't where it was supposed to be, the chances of finding it were pretty much nil. But she had to try. Dmitri had warned her that the location was approximate.

She had worked her way through most of the file cabinets, yanking and slamming through them like a secretary on steroids, when something made her freeze and stand in absolute silence. A sound. The sound of someone opening the door of the agency even though the gate was down. There was no time to wonder how the hell that could happen. With lightning speed she leapt up to the top of one of the file cabinets and climbed back into the ventilation system, peering out to see what would happen next.

The woman who'd been behind the desk came into the room, along with two men. All of the woman's spacey disorganization was completely gone. She even looked different—she moved with athletic agility as she went to her desk and cleared a few things out of the top drawer.

The two men with her were of average height but were also powerfully compact. One sported a mustache, the other wore a baseball cap, and all three moved silently to separate desks. They were almost choreographed, their moves were so organized, like they had trained for this moment.

"I don't know how this happened," Gray Lady muttered in irritation. "This location has been under the radar for so long. I don't know how our secrecy got compromised."

"It lasted longer than it was supposed to," Mustache Guy said, moving a heavy object—Gaia couldn't see what—to the center of the room from just outside the door.

"It's just part of the deal," Mr. Hat said. "I hate when this happens, though. It gives me the creeps. I feel like someone's watching me right now. Let's get the stuff we're supposed to save and get the hell out of here."

"Keep your shirt on," Gray Lady said. "Okay, I'm ready."

Before she even completed the sentence, Gaia heard something being poured methodically around the room, and the pungent odor of gasoline hit her nostrils just as she realized what was happening. These Organization operatives were destroying this front as part of a random cleanup operation. In other words, the place was about to go up in smoke. She had to get out of there!

The agents left through the door, letting themselves out whichever way they had come, and Gaia heard the *whup* of the fire as the gasoline flamed under the match they dropped.

Tubes in and out of my body.

An upside-down bag hung next to my bed. Faces of women. Concern. Where am I?

I think I hear sobbing. Is it real or in my head? Television. I hear a television. Canned laughter rolling in waves. Over and over again. New jokes, old laughs. Hahaha.

Someone's finger moves. I see a ring finger flick upward in a sort of spasm. Is that on purpose? It's mine. That's my finger. This is my body. I'm in a. . .

Everything is so streamlined. My vision is dim. Is it a spaceship?

I can't move. Even my eyes—I can't seem to move my eyes around the room. They stare out from beneath drooping eyelids, neither open nor closed. They blink automatically. My throat swallows at regular intervals. The nurses come and go.

Nurses. I'm in a hospital. I'm in a hospital and I hear nurses. They sound like they are at a great distance.

Everything is at a great distance.

I see my brother, Tom. I see his beautiful girlfriend sitting with me on the steps of Low Library. There is a place we go to eat, the West End.

Katia. Her face is so sad, as if she knows something that is going to happen to me. As if she knows what has happened to me.

I seem to be in a coma. I can't make sense of any of this. Who is Gaia? Why does her name float around and around in my mind like a mantra?

I become tired easily. I make an effort to speak. I feel like I am shouting, but nobody hears me because my lips stubbornly refuse to move, my vocal cords frozen, cut off from the words my mind screams out.

Some of the nurses are kind. They treat me like a beloved houseplant. I'm not.

I'm Oliver Moore. I want to wake up, and I can't.

Maybe he was
surprised
just to see **failed**
her without
a body **mission**
bag and
toe tag.

DESPITE THE YELLOW FOLDER IN HER

Steamy Bathroom

lap, Gaia sat on the subway as it lurched through the tunnels, feeling like the lowest form of life. She'd been given an assignment and had only completed half of it. Worse, the assignment had been integral to her finding her father; she had totally failed him already, and her search had just begun. She tried not to let it get her down—even Babe Ruth didn't always hit a home run, right?—but it was no use. Maybe if she'd searched the drawers quicker, or started from the other end, or stopped to think logically about where else it could have been. . .

She knew where it was now. In a pile of waterlogged, smoking ashes being shoveled out of a busted-up storefront by the NYFD. Fat lot of good it was going to do her.

As her train pulled into the Grand Street stop, she began to worry. She was angry at Dmitri for not giving her more detailed information. How could he have been so right and specific about the Places of Interest folder—and so grossly wrong about the Tom Moore folder? What was it about the travel folder that was so important? And where was he getting his information?

But she squelched her questions. The fact was, she

didn't have what she had set out to get, and he could easily be angry with her for not finding the folder, with or without his directions. She was in a knot of worry and tension over her failed mission. It was all she could think about as she made her way to Dmitri's building on Forsyth Street.

As she lifted her hand to press the buzzer on Dmitri's door, Gaia realized that she had made a terrible mistake. She couldn't go up to Dmitri's. What if Sam was there? She couldn't face him. Not after he'd tried to kill her.

She buzzed again.

"Yes?" Dmitri sounded impatient.

"I need to know that you're alone," she said. "I want to know that nobody is up there with you. Nobody."

"I sent Sam for a walk," Dmitri answered, as if he'd known she'd ask for privacy. She sighed with relief. *Good old guy,* she thought. *Smart old guy.* He buzzed again, and this time she pushed through the door and ran up the four flights of stairs.

Dmitri's door was unlocked and open. Gaia walked through it and shoved it closed behind her, flicking the dead bolt. The old man was in the green-walled kitchen, dipping a tea bag up and down in a tall glass, clinking it against the spoon that stood in its darkening depths.

"Here's your folder," she said, plopping it on the table. Dmitri didn't look up.

"You are as skilled and powerful as they said you were." He sighed, shaking his head. "I knew you could do this, my dear girl. Please sit, and I will make you a nice hot tea."

"I don't want a nice hot anything," Gaia told him. "I've had enough heat for one day. The Organization destroyed their front before I could finish the job. They set it on fire."

That woke Dmitri from his meditative tea making. "What? My child, are you all right?" He looked up, and his face took on an expression of concern. For the first time he noticed what a mess she was, and Gaia saw herself reflected in his reaction. Her hair torn and matted. Her skin caked with dust and muck. Her jeans gray and her sneakers half melted. Ugh. No wonder people had kept their distance on the subway. She either looked like a crazy person or an extra from the newest Christina Aguilera video.

"Oh, my dear, I had no idea—how could I have let you go?" Dmitri asked, squeezing her upper arms and patting her face with concern. "I would never have sent you if I had known they were planning such an action."

"I don't know who you got your information from, but whoever it is might be trying to set you up," Gaia told him. "Not only were they planning on destroying the place. . . there was another problem, too."

"What?"

Gaia forced herself to spit out the bad news. "The dossier on my father wasn't where it was supposed to be," she said. "I found the right file cabinet, and there were files in there similar to the one you said I'd find, but none was labeled *Moorestown,* and none contained information about him. I was in the process of checking out the rest of the file cabinets when the Organization operatives came back to destroy the place." She paused. "I'm sorry."

The old man's face fell as she relayed the story. He shook his head and sank into a chair, looking even older than he had when they'd found him.

"Dmitri, are you okay?" He was looking distinctly ashen. Gaia thought he might be having a stroke or something.

"I feel terrible," he said. "I put you in danger for an empty reason. Perhaps you are right—I am too feeble-minded to help you find your father."

Gaia sat next to him at the table. "Here, drink your tea," she told him. He gave her a sad stare, and she pushed the tea closer to him. He took a sip, grimaced, then took a sugar cube out of a tin on the table and put it between his front teeth, then sipped again, and then a few more times. His color seemed to return a little bit.

Frail as he was, he was Gaia's best hope of finding her father: Even if fifty percent of his information were flawed, it was more than she was going to find anywhere else. Whether or not she trusted this guy, she had to keep the information coming.

"Don't worry about it," she said. "My dad used to tell me that was part of any kind of information gathering. You have to know that a lot of it is going to come up short. You get what you can and don't give up if it's not what you expect." She genuinely felt bad for Dmitri. She hated to see him blame himself, even though she'd been blaming him just a short while earlier. Funny how that happened. She was relieved to see him nod in response.

"That is true," he said. "I know it is true, but I wish I had not endangered your life for such a slim chance at finding what we need."

"It's okay. Does this folder have to do with my father?" she asked, tapping the yellow folder.

"Only indirectly," Dmitri said. "I need to go through the information and decode what is there. It is possible that there will be locations of other prisons and cells, and from there I can investigate to see if there has been movement recently that might indicate his arrival in one of them. But it is working backward. The other file would have led us directly to him."

Gaia felt a pang of regret. Once again, the crappy option had won. But there was nothing she could do about it now.

"Please, I would like you to clean up," Dmitri told her. "You must have a shower and let me wash your clothes. This apartment has a small washing machine and dryer."

"This place?" Gaia looked around.

"It was outfitted so that operatives like myself could stay inside for long periods of time." He shrugged. "I believe the addition of females to our ranks encouraged some creature comforts."

"Huh." Gaia had to admit, a shower sounded good. But she really didn't want to run into Sam. "No, I've got to go," she said.

"I insist," Dmitri said firmly. "Sam will not be back for a long time. I don't know why you wouldn't want to see him, but it's obvious that you don't. Please, don't let that stand in the way of your taking care of yourself."

Jeez, this guy was such a mother hen. "All right," Gaia relented. "I'll take a quick shower. I'd probably attract too much attention on the street looking like this, anyway."

"I'll turn on the hot water now," Dmitri said. "It takes a long time to warm up."

A few minutes later Gaia stood in the steamy bathroom, inspecting the damage to herself. She looked like absolute hell. There was an old brush sitting on the sink, and she tried to yank it through her hair. Giving up, she stepped into the warm stream of water and let the heat sink into her muscles. It burned where the fire had gotten too close. But it felt too good to stop. Forgetting herself, she relaxed and stood with her eyes closed for a long, long time.

SAM SAT IN THE PUBLIC LIBRARY,

Hidden Masses

reading through the newspapers from the time that he'd been gone and trying to catch up on what he'd missed. He was tired of being a shadow in this world. And though he knew he had to hide—well, that was one of the things about New York that could be either great or horrible, depending on how depressed you were. You could be hidden in plain sight. The city was full of people who might as well be invisible. Old people with no way to fill their empty hours, young people with no direction or desire, displaced people waiting for the next adventure or catastrophe—they filled the public places, the parks and atriums and subways, and even this library.

And Sam fit right in with the hidden masses.

He just wanted to know what was going on. Paging through recent papers and magazines and flicking through microfilm was sort of soothing and reassuring. He followed the case of a city scandal about misdirected funds and the dog pound. Totally boring to most, but it was one more thread pulling Sam's consciousness together. He followed a celebrity divorce from bitter feud to conciliatory appearance on the red carpet. Another thread. He skimmed the top choices of a daytime show's book club. Whatever he could get his hands on, anything that could tell him what had happened in the world during his confinement, Sam gobbled up with greed. He couldn't explain why he had such a craving for information. The only reason he could think of was that he just wanted to make up for lost time. To re-create the world as it rolled on without him so he wouldn't have this massive blank spot in his worldview.

All that reading made Sam tired. He was still physically drained from his injuries—and the stress on his body wasn't helping his diabetes, either. He marveled at the fact that his captors had treated him so badly—neglected his every need—but had managed to get him the insulin he needed to survive. As if they wanted him to live, but with a broken spirit. Well, today's research mission had taken him a long way toward repairing that spirit.

But damn, his body still needed some mending.

As he hopped on the subway and headed back

down to Chinatown, Sam noticed with a rush that he hadn't thought about Gaia in hours. Not that she wasn't there—but she hadn't been in the forefront of his mind. She was starting to shrink from the massive icon in his mind into regular old Gaia Moore, high school girl who had stolen his heart.

Funny thing, though. His heart still tightened at the thought of her. His temperature still spiked when he pictured the way her hands brushed across his chest. He still had the most massive feelings for her. Even shrunk down to normal size, Gaia still ruled Sam's heart.

And damn it, between misplacing his cell phone, Dmitri's Internet habit, and the lack of working public phones in this city, he hadn't been able to get in touch with her all morning. Couldn't even comfort her—as a friend—after her fight with Ed. It drove him crazy. But that was the way it was.

The last thing he expected, as he exited the train and walked up to Dmitri's apartment, was to see the object of his desire, obsessive or otherwise, wrapped in a terry cloth robe with her hair swathed in a turbaned towel. Even in his fantasies, he hadn't thought he'd walk into the dingy apartment to find Gaia Moore dripping wet and basically naked. In fact, a postshower Gaia was the last thing Sam Moon had expected to find as he opened the door to Dmitri's apartment and trudged toward his room.

"OH! GOD!" GAIA YELPED AS SHE came out of the bathroom to ask Dmitri what he'd done with her clothes. *Stupid, stupid, STUPID,* she thought. Her heart felt like it had just exploded inside her chest, leaving pulsating bits of arterial matter splattered all over her lungs and stomach. All the

End of Story

warm relaxation of the hot shower drained from her body as she came face-to-face with Sam Moon.

Sam, the guy she still had lingering feelings for. Sam, the guy who had apparently arranged for her murder the night before. Part of her still bloomed with happiness at the sight of that handsome face; the rest of her wilted with disgust at the guy who'd set her up to be whacked. With all the breaking and entering and arson of the afternoon, she had forgotten her resolution to get out of Dmitri's apartment before Sam got back.

Because this was more than she could stand to think about right now.

"Gaia! Are you all right?" Sam seemed surprised and thrilled to see her—tried to hug her, in fact. Maybe he was checking for the bullet holes that were supposed to be there. Maybe he was surprised just to see her without a body bag and toe tag. Or maybe she was wrong and he hadn't set her up.

Click. Her mind turned off and her instincts

switched on. Gaia had to get out of this claustrophobic apartment, and pronto.

"Sam, you are back early," Dmitri said with dismay, appearing behind him with Gaia's clothes, cleaned and folded.

"I thought nobody would be here," Gaia said to him. "I thought our discussion was top secret."

"It is," Dmitri told her. "He only just walked in. Why are you so upset?"

"I'm not upset," Gaia snapped, taking her clothes and vanishing back into the bathroom. "I'm just mad that I hung out this long," she called out through the door as she frantically shoved her still damp legs into her jeans. *Mmm, that's a pretty feeling: wet denim is just sooo comfortable,* she noted distractedly. She did not care. She had to get out of there.

Of all the idiotic moves, she scolded herself. *Getting sidetracked by a shower. Running into Sam when you have to stay focused on your dad. Some reliable daughter you are.* She barely noticed how melted her sneakers were as she shoved her feet into them and twisted her hair into a waterlogged knot on top of her head.

She left the bathroom in a rush, heading straight for the front door as if she were a racehorse with blinders on. "Let me know what you found in that file," she called out to Dmitri.

"Gaia," Sam said uncertainly.

"Yeah?" She paused at the door, her hand on the

knob. She felt her heart take a swan dive into her small intestine, bouncing on her pancreas, liver, and stomach on its way down. Sam's presence loomed like a planet behind her.

"Are—are you okay?" he asked. "The last time I saw you, you were fighting with Ed. I just wanted to make sure things worked out."

Are you kidding me? Gaia shrieked inside her head. *Ed's not exactly primo in my mind right now, Mister Killing-Me-Not-So-Softly.* But she didn't want to let on that she suspected him. *Let him wonder why I'm not dead for a while,* she decided. *Confront him later, when you've got more evidence.*

"Everything's fine," she said stonily, glaring at the doorknob. "Can't you see for yourself? I'm in one piece."

With that parting shot, she yanked open the door and left the apartment. *Ha,* she thought. *Let him chew on that for a while.* She felt a certain satisfaction that her thinly veiled insult might dig into his double-crossing soul and show him that he couldn't eliminate her so easily.

Of course, it was hard to ignore the fact that the look on his face had been more baffled and hurt than insulted and evil.

But ignore it she did. He'd sent the message that brought her to the church. And in that church she'd been shot at and very nearly killed. End of story.

Right?

Right. *Right!*

94

Even in the
life of
Gaia, this **stark**
was a **contrast**
weird one.

CROSSING THROUGH THE PARK AGAIN,

Gaia felt her head reeling from the potent cocktail of Sam-induced hormones, dad-inspired guilt, and Dmitri-assisted annoyance. She just wanted to wiggle out of her skin like a snake and leave her old self behind. *Everything is such a mess,* she thought. *All I want to do is find my dad, and the harder I try, the more everything in my life gets more screwed up.*

Shoop-Shoop

Calling it a park was generous. Let's get real: To get to the subway, all Gaia had to get through was a half-block-wide strip of grass between two avenues at the base of the Manhattan Bridge. There wasn't much room for a lanky, athletic girl loping along in a blind fury. Predictably, Gaia collided with one of a group of geriatric Chinese people practicing t'ai chi.

"I'm sorry," she blurted out. Expecting to see an elderly Chinese lady glaring up at her, she was both relieved and confused when the victim of her klutziness turned out to be Jake.

"What the hell are you doing here?" she asked.

Jake lay on his back, looking just as startled and confused. "Gaia? Did you just try to mug me?"

Gaia let out an exasperated breath. "Yeah, I was trying to mug you," she spat. "Times are tough, you know. A girl needs her lunch money." Then she stepped over his prone frame and stomped up the street. What a day she was having. Even in the life of Gaia, this was a weird one.

"Gaia!" Jake stood and chased after her, dusting himself off as he went. "I was just kidding. Would you stop?"

"What do you want?" she snapped.

"I was just—jeez! Come on, Gaia, don't you think it's kind of funny that you literally ran into me in a totally different part of town?"

Gaia stood for a moment, glaring at him.

"Ha ha," she finally said. "Can I leave now?"

"No!" Jake scratched his head and looked at her curiously. "Are you okay? I mean, you're not exactly the friendliest person on a normal day, but you're acting really weird."

"Why, because I don't want to sit and chat with you?"

"No. Because you literally just knocked me over and you didn't even say excuse me. You're such a weirdo!"

Jake was still laughing, and it was making Gaia feel strange. Besides, the word *weirdo* was echoing in her head in a way it never had before. Ed's fault. He'd made that crack about how she couldn't be part of anything. Okay, so he hadn't actually made that crack; Gaia had just inferred it from the way he was looking at her. But it still snowballed with Jake's current crack enough to make Gaia stop herself from storming off.

"Sorry," she said. "I was in a hurry."

"Well, will you slow down?" he asked. "At least long

enough so I can save face with Mrs. Ong and her lady friends?"

Gaia looked over and saw the small crowd of `still gently swaying t'ai chi people`. A few of them, though they still had expressions of serene distraction, were peeking over between moves. Jake waved at them, like he was trying to be a little less embarrassed.

"You're friends with these old people?" Gaia blurted out.

"Well, I come down here sometimes just to watch them do their thing," he said. "Karate isn't the only stuff I do. The guy who teaches me said I should be familiar with yoga, t'ai chi, and whatever else I can scare up." He looked back at the swaying figures. "I keep wanting to join in, but I feel funny."

"Yeah, so would I," Gaia told him. "You'd kind of stick out. You're about two feet taller than any of them, for one thing."

"But they keep saying I should join in. I think if I had a partner, I'd feel a little better." He peered at her. She glared back.

"No," she said.

"I didn't ask yet," he objected.

"Fine, ask."

"Will you come do some t'ai chi with me and the old people so I won't feel so self-conscious?"

"*No.*"

"Gaia!" Jake shook his head.

Is this guy just relentlessly amused by every stupid thing that happens on the planet? Gaia wondered. *Just what is so goddamn funny?*

"Come on. Have you ever tried it?"

"When I was a kid," Gaia admitted. "And I did some yoga, too. But karate's more my style. I'm not really into deep inner calm."

"Trust me, neither is Mrs. Ong," Jake said. "The first time I met her, she was throwing a fish at someone."

Gaia laughed in spite of herself. She had to admit, the willowy movements of the serene oldsters looked very cool. Plus they all seemed to be absolutely free of the kind of anger and frustration that was turning her stomach into a bucket of acid.

"I suppose it could make me a better fighter," she admitted.

"Sure. Focus and whatnot," Jake agreed. "Help you stay cool in a hot situation, reducing that panic response most people get in the middle of a fight. Fear's a killer, you know."

"I've heard that," Gaia said.

"Come on," Jake wheedled, dropping his messenger bag at his feet. "I've always wanted to try this. We're so far from school, nobody will spot us."

People from school weren't the issue. Gaia peered up at Dmitri's building. His apartment was on the other side; she wasn't likely to be spotted by him or by

Sam. And it wasn't like she was in a hurry to get back to her Tatiana-infested apartment. This day had her totally frazzled. She hated to admit it, but Jake could be right: Something calming might be just what she needed to grab hold of herself and refocus her attention on the search for her dad.

"All right, I'll try it," Gaia said. "But the minute I start feeling stupid, I'm out of here."

"It's a deal," Jake said.

They joined the group in the middle of the park, imitating the poses of the people in front of them as they moved through a slow-motion series of stances that went back thousands and thousands of years. A lot of them were similar to the ones Gaia knew from martial arts training, but holding them and moving through them at superslow speed made her feel weirdly calm. Her muscles seemed to really enjoy it, and she felt the whirling gyroscope of her brain begin to slow to a comfortable hum. After a few minutes the two of them stopped, stepped out from the huddle of people, and walked slowly up the street.

Gaia didn't really feel like talking. She didn't want to break the silence in her head. She remembered this feeling from scuba diving: After coming up to the surface, even the biggest motormouths tended to just sit in a blissful daze. The shoop-shoop breathing sounds of the deep lulled everyone into a waking sleep. She felt that way now, too.

Apparently Jake felt the same way. He was just strolling along, eyes cast downward, in as meditative a silence as she was. He looked up and smiled, still not speaking. Gaia didn't go so far as to smile back, but she didn't feel the need to scowl at him and look away, either.

Well. This was nice. No accusations, no arguing, no betrayal, no weirdness. *Maybe all I needed was to get away from everyone,* Gaia mused. *Everyone I'm usually around, anyway.*

"So where did you learn to fight?" Jake asked her as they walked toward the F train.

"Oh. . . I don't know."

"Come on. Of course you know," Jake pressed.

Gaia shrugged. "It was just something I got really into when I was a kid," she told him.

"Uh, no." Jake shook his head. "If it was just a hobby, you wouldn't have such professional-level skills. What are you really? One of those circus kids? Like Jackie Chan? Did a traveling martial arts circus take you away from your parents at the age of three and mold you into a killer?"

Gaia laughed. That made twice in one day, she noted. "It wasn't quite that dramatic," she nonanswered, sidestepping the question. "What about you?"

"Oh, I got interested the way every other red-blooded American does," he told her. "By seeing a Bruce Lee movie with my older brother at an impressionable age. After that, I had to do it. I guess I was

101

kind of a weird kid because I never got tired of it, never gave it up, even when we got Nintendo."

"Wow, you stuck with it even in the face of impending Sonic the Hedgehog," Gaia said dryly. "Who knew anyone could resist temptation like that?"

"Damn, you're harsh!" Jake laughed. Gaia shot him a withering look. "You're so different from everyone else at school," he added, almost as an afterthought.

You don't know the half of it, Gaia thought. "I do seem to stand out," she mumbled.

"Look, I know you think I'm a meathead or something," Jake said, stopping in the middle of the Houston Street sidewalk. "Or maybe you haven't given me much thought at all. All I know is, you absolutely refuse to respond to my friendly advances, which no one has ever done before."

Gaia smirked. "You're very fond of yourself, aren't you?" she asked.

"Not really," Jake answered. "I just want to hang out some more. I think you're very. . . interesting. It seems like you have a lot more going on here than you let on," he added, putting his hand on his heart when he said the word *here.*

What was he suggesting? That under Gaia's tough demeanor was some fragile waif waiting for someone to unlock her heart? Was he for real?

"Look, that's very touching and all, but I really don't have a whole lot going on *here,*" she said as she put her own hand on her heart, mocking his previous gesture.

"Oh, I think you do," Jake said, this time putting his hand on *her* heart. "I can feel it," he said.

Now he was way out of line. Simply put, Jake was playing to the wrong audience.

"Hey—careful with the merchandise," Gaia said, swatted his hand away.

"Okay, sorry. I didn't mean to upset you," Jake said. "I won't do it again."

Gaia wasn't exactly sure what was going on in Jake's head. Was he flirting with her, or was he just trying to reach out and fix someone? Either way, Gaia was in no position to add any more names to the already too long list of people in her life.

"Look, I have to go," Gaia said.

Jake looked hurt and bewildered. "Gaia, don't leave. I promise not to come near you again."

"It's not that," Gaia said. "I just have to be somewhere."

Gaia hurried away from Jake, taking long strides down the sidewalk and feeling just as agitated as ever. God! She should never have done t'ai chi. It had relaxed her so much, she'd let down her defenses and opened herself up to yet another attack—of sorts. Right now she didn't need to be introspective or calm or serene. And she certainly didn't need to open her heart. She needed to stay on her guard, listen for bullets whistling past her head, and get things done.

What things, she didn't know. But she had to get things done.

BY THE TIME SHE GOT BACK TO THE Upper East Side, Gaia had calmed down somewhat, but she was still in no mood to be messed with. She was glad she had been able to avoid a confrontation with Sam. She felt like an idiot over Jake. And she felt sad about Ed. All in all, her emotions were still a complete jumble, but at least she was blocks and blocks away from anyone who could—

Squeezed and Crushed

"Gaia."

Oh.

That voice drizzled over Gaia's heart like honey over a piece of toast. She turned around.

"Didn't I just leave you downtown, Sam?" she asked, trying not to look up at him. She had to keep herself safe. And noticing how rumpled and handsome he was—that was about as unsafe as it got. *He tried to kill you,* she reminded herself. That helped. A little.

"Well, yeah." He stood in her way, not moving.

"You did. But I couldn't let you walk away like that. Gaia, what is going on?"

"Nothing's going on," she mumbled. She tried to walk past him, but he wasn't budging.

"The last time I saw you was right here," he pointed out. "Right in front of your building. You were arguing with Ed. And I think it's partially my fault. I've been pushing myself on you and taking up your time. I hope he wasn't too angry at you."

"We broke up," she told him.

"Oh, Gaia. I'm so sorry." Sam made a move to hug her. Gaia stepped back. She was starting to get really steamed. It was painful, seeing how Sam could lie to her face like this. *He tried to kill you,* she reminded herself again. But this time it didn't help her feel better. It fueled her anger.

"It's okay," she said. "I mean, it was a long time coming. It's not your fault. Not anyone's fault. You should go back to Dmitri's."

"Look, what is your deal?" Sam was getting angry. "I'm just trying to be a friend, and you've put up the Great Wall of Gaia. Is something bigger going on? Is it something with your dad or—all this other stuff that's happening?"

"I can't believe you!" Gaia finally exploded. Her anger rose like vomit into the back of her throat. "How dare you talk to me like you give a crap about my well-being? Why don't you get the hell out of my life?"

105

Sam's face seemed to melt, from confusion to horri-fied incredulity. "Wha-what are you talking about?" he stammered. The old habit came out when he was under stress. Gaia was amazed he could fake it like that.

"You set me up, Sam. You tried to have me killed. Did you think I was too stupid to put two and two together? Here's a hint: When you've been that sloppy, you've got to finish the job or the girl you're trying to murder's going to be *really mad*." The words rolled out of Gaia's mouth. Not even his expression of complete and utter noncomprehension could stop her.

"Set you up? Have you killed? Gaia, I don't—"

Gaia whipped out her cell phone and shoved it in his face. "I've still got the text message you sent me," she pointed out, scrolling it up on the screen. "From your cell phone to mine, courtesy of Smith and Wesson."

Sam took the phone out of her hands and looked at the screen.

Don't be sad. Just received some new information. Meet me at the Ukrainian church on Eleventh Street. Tomorrow. 8:00 A.M.

"Oh my God. Gaia, I did not send this to you." The words tumbled out of Sam, who was staring at the cell phone with horrified shock. "I couldn't have. My cell phone has been missing since I left your apartment."

"Yeah, right," Gaia said. "I got the message like five seconds. . . after you left," she said, finishing her sen-tence in a self-doubting whisper.

No. No more doubt, she told herself. *You can't trust him. You can't trust anyone.*

"You're just saying that because I busted you," she insisted, snatching the phone back. "I know you tried to kill me, Sam. Now you want to talk your way out of it, and you can't. Just leave me alone." She pushed past him, feeling doubt nagging at her, tugging on her sleeve like an insistent child.

"Gaia—"

"I'm serious." She whipped around. "Just—leave me alone. I have to find my dad. I'll deal with you later."

Gaia blocked out the memory of Sam's confused, pained expression the minute she turned her back on him and went into her building. Her feelings for Sam were as intense as ever. But she couldn't ignore the message and its aftermath. She felt like a palm tree getting thrown around by a hurricane. *You bend this way, you bend that way, but that doesn't mean you can't break,* she thought. The confusion and emotion inside her were like a tourniquet around her heart. She felt squeezed and crushed. The pain was physical, and it was intense.

She took a moment in the elevator to shut her eyes and focus. Sam was not her problem. Finding her father was. She breathed deeply, forcing her heart to slow and her temperature to drop. By the time she entered the apartment, she had managed to push Sam to the back of her mind. She thought she'd lie down and try to figure out what to do next or just wait for Dmitri's next word.

Hearing a noise, she walked warily to the living room. There was Natasha, sitting on the bloodred velvet couch, folding laundry in a huge wicker basket.

"Natasha!" Gaia said, surprised. She had to admit, it was a relief to see someone familiar. Natasha was as close as she could get to her dad, after all. "I didn't think I'd find you here."

"Well, I do live here," the older woman responded.

"But you've been gone. Where were you?" Gaia sat next to her, thinking of the way Tatiana sat next to her mother, trying to imitate the same ease.

"Terribly busy," she said. "There has been much to do in searching for your father."

"You look tired," Gaia told her. It was true. Natasha's willowy, elegant frame looked as young as ever, but her face had a completely different cast to it than it had just a few days before. Gaia felt a swell of affection for her. It hadn't been easy, getting used to having a stepmother. But she believed her dad really loved this woman. The brief moment that they'd all been a family had already taken on the golden glow of nostalgia.

"Well, I guess I have been worried," Natasha admitted, putting down the socks she'd been rolling and resting her long, white fingers against her eyes, the red nails at her fingertips standing out in stark contrast to her pale skin.

"What did you find out?" Gaia asked.

"You know I cannot tell you that," Natasha told her sternly.

"Of course you can. You have to," Gaia insisted. "He's my father."

"I know, but there are professionals handling this. You have to have faith that we know what we are doing."

"Faith?" Gaia gave a frustrated roar. "Look, no offense, but it was you people who thought George Niven would keep me safe, and I almost got iced by him and his trashy wife."

"I know, I know," Natasha said. "That was regrettable, but I am telling you, the search for your father is being handled."

"Don't you get updates? I mean, aren't you his fiancée? Should I contact them directly? As a blood relative, I mean. Maybe I'll get more out of them."

"They hate that." Natasha shook her head. "No, we are supposed to be good soldiers and hold our positions until we get different orders. I am sure they have everything under control."

"Natasha! Will you stop saying that?" Gaia took a pair of socks from Natasha's hands and threw them on the floor. "My father almost choked and died. I'd say there's a pretty good chance he was poisoned. He was taken to a hospital, where he just. . . vanished. And all you want to do is sit here waiting for orders? I thought you *loved* him."

"I do love him," Natasha said firmly, fixing Gaia with a sharp glare. She stared at her for a long time, with an odd expression that Gaia couldn't quite read.

"Please," Gaia said. "Tell me whatever you know."

Natasha dropped her eyes. "The truth is, I am being stonewalled, too," she finally admitted. "I cannot. . ." She seemed to wrench the words out of herself. "I cannot seem to get a straight answer from our superiors. They tell me that he is alive but that he is being kept in a remote location."

"Which is where?"

"I do not know. They say the less I know, the safer I will be." She raised her eyes to look into Gaia's. "The same is true for you, Gaia. Obviously something terribly dangerous—more dangerous than anything we've faced before—is going on. We must be in danger. I think it is best to keep a low profile for now."

Gaia sat still, trying to take all of this in. Natasha was a trusted operative—and her own organization wouldn't tell her where her fiancé was?

"This is okay with you?" Gaia said. "I don't understand why you'd accept that answer. Didn't you press it?"

"I pressed. And I got nowhere."

Gaia sat back on the couch, deflated.

"Your father is in good hands—I am sure of it," Natasha told her. "If he comes back—I mean, when he comes back"—Natasha gave Gaia an apologetic shake of her head—"he will appreciate that we did not endanger our own lives to find him. He wants you safe, Gaia. Even if it means there's one less person searching for him."

Gaia scowled. "I don't think I can just sit here," she said. "And I'm trying to understand how you can." She stood and started to leave the living room.

"Gaia."

She stopped but didn't turn around.

"I know that Tatiana threw a party here last night. She should not have done that, and I have spoken to her about it. Especially when we are all so worried about your father. I think perhaps the stress is getting to her. Perhaps she is not being the most responsible person right now. I hope you will not be too impatient with her."

Gaia nodded, then kept walking. Stress. Stress had made Tatiana get totally drunk and blab about her friendship with Sam to Ed? *If I dealt with stress that badly, I'd never have made it this far,* Gaia thought. But she didn't want to start another conversation with Natasha. This one had made her too sad and confused.

She went to her bedroom. Before she even hit the door, she could hear tapping at the computer keyboard. She steeled herself to see Tatiana and hoped she wouldn't be—

Ed.

Ed was sitting at the desk, not Tatiana.

"What are you doing here?" she asked, standing uncomfortably by the door.

Ed looked up and seemed thoroughly resigned to the fact that he and Gaia were within ten feet of each other.

"Sorry," he said. "I had to do some stuff for Tatiana, and I didn't think you'd come home. I'll be out of here soon."

"No, it's okay," Gaia said. "I'll just go. I was heading back out, anyway."

"Wait."

A pause. "What?"

"I just—I mean, why don't you just hang out? I'll be done soon." He met her eyes for about half a millisecond. "There's no reason we shouldn't be able to hang out in the same room, Gaia."

She thought about that one. There were a few reasons. The totally harsh way he'd spoken to her, for one thing. The fact that he used to be the safest person in the world to her and that they had just broken up about ten seconds before. And she didn't know how to act around him. Because she couldn't even blame him for being mad at her, because she hadn't exactly been forthcoming or truthful with him. There were a lot of reasons why they couldn't really hang out.

Then again, he was Ed. What was she scared of? He was just Ed. Gaia sat on the edge of her bed farthest from her ex-boyfriend, ex–best friend, ex-everything.

"So what are you doing?" she asked.

"Tatiana asked me to burn some CDs for her, so I figured I'd Limewire some extra stuff and make her a mix."

"Hm."

Another pause. These pauses were getting really annoying. What had once been a comfortable silence now seemed like a screaming chasm of unspoken words.

"What?" Ed asked.

"Nothing."

"No, you said, 'Hm.'"

"Yeah, I mean, hm, so you're making some CDs, that's nice. Whatever."

"Whatever?"

"Yeah, whatever."

Ed poked a couple of keys to set the CD burner running and put his hands in his lap.

"Look, I know what you're thinking," he said.

"Really? Mind reading is quite a talent. Maybe you should go on *Letterman*," Gaia tried to joke.

"I'm serious. I know you feel weird about me and Tatiana, and I just. . ."

What, Ed? You just want me to know you're considering getting close to my roommate and almost stepsister? You just want to put my weird feelings out in the open so I can feel even weirder? Gaia wondered.

"I just—I'm not planning on going out with her," he finally said. "We're just friends."

"I don't care, Ed. I mean, it's fine. We're not together, so I can't tell you what to do."

"Well, if you don't care," Ed said, rolling his eyes to the ceiling. "I mean, I think you do."

"But it doesn't matter." The words came out more forcefully than Gaia intended. She was telling herself as much as she was telling Ed. And neither one of them was really buying it. So she said it again. "It doesn't matter," she said. "Tatiana's got her eye on you. Things didn't work out between us. If she's being a good friend, then why should I object?"

"I just don't know why you couldn't be—I don't know, more like she is," Ed blurted out. Gaia's eyes widened as she felt a wiggle of misery worming its way around her heart.

"I don't mean not to be yourself, but it's frustrating," he clarified. "I mean, you and I were best friends for, like, ever, but when I look back on all the time we spent together, I can count on one hand the number of times you just up and did something unexpected just because you were thinking of me."

"That's not true. I thought of you a lot," Gaia objected. "I just had other stuff going on. Some of the time. Okay, I mean, a lot of the time."

"*All* of the time." Ed shook his head, checked on the CD, and turned toward Gaia. "I'm not saying this to piss you off, but man, you might want to think about it for next time."

Next time what? Next time I have a boyfriend? Always-thinkin'-ahead Ed. "And you and I were great friends, but just look at all the stuff Tatiana does for me. I just mentioned in passing that I like cannolis, and voilà, today she brings me a cannoli from this place." He dropped a half-empty bag from Veniero's, a well-known pastry shop in the East Village, on the bed. "And look, this goofy bobble-head dog from Pearl River Trading."

"I mean, Ed."

"What?"

"The dog is kind of dorky. It's just a five-dollar trinket from Chinatown."

"I know!" Ed threw his hands in the air. "But it's nice! It's nice to have someone think about me for a change instead of me always wondering about—about you, and whether you like me or why you're ignoring me or when we're going to hang out again. Tatiana went all the way down to Eleventh Street, for no reason other than to be nice."

Ugh! Every word he said felt like a hornet in Gaia's heart. She *did* care about him! She wanted to yell it out loud. *I thought about you!* she yelled inside. *All I did was think about you. You and your safety were more important to me than I was to myself. You think it was easy avoiding you all that time and making you hate me? It was pure torture, but I did it because I love you.*

She couldn't say any of that. It was too embarrassing to admit, even to Ed. It left her too exposed. And anyway, what was the point? He was finished with her.

"Well, so that's great," she said. "You've got what you wanted."

"Gaia." Ed leaned back and stared at the wall. The complete and utter aggravation of trying to get his point across to Gaia was starting to exhaust him completely.

"It's what I wanted, but it's not who I wanted it from," he said. "I wanted it from. . . Gaia?"

He finally managed to look over, wanting to meet Gaia's eyes as he admitted how he really felt. But all he saw was an empty white wall next to an open door. The front door slammed. Gaia was gone.

This is just weird. I don't—it doesn't make sense. Veniero's on Eleventh Street—that's right across the avenue from the Ukranian church where I almost got my head shot off. Pearl River? That's in Chinatown—by Dmitri's apartment. By Sam's apartment. The cell phone. The last time I saw it, it was here, and Tatiana was standing three feet away. Drunk as a skunk, but still. . .

Or was she? I remember a story about Nikita Kruschev, the prime minister of the Soviet Union during the Cold War. He was at a big diplomatic party, and he was getting drunker and drunker. Then someone smelled his drink, and it turned out he wasn't drinking straight vodka, as he'd claimed. It was just water, and he was trying to catch everyone off their guard. Thinking they'd give away government secrets if they thought he was too drunk to notice. A sneaky little trick.

Could Tatiana have heard the

same story? Was she pretending to be drunk so that she could steal the cell phone?

Bigger picture: Is this loving mother-daughter team nothing more than a couple of double agents setting me up to get killed?

That was my first instinct about them. When I met them, I just didn't trust them. But they hung in there with me. They really did. And besides, my dad trusts Natasha. Enough to fall in love with her. Enough to leave me in her care. That's the bottom line, right? He taught me everything I know. He did something unbeliev-ably difficult—disappeared from my life—just because he thought it would keep me safe. Even though it made me hate him. Even though he had to fight to get me to under-stand. And that guy, the one who did all that—he trusts Natasha. So I should, too, shouldn't I?

These signs—these tiny clues and these little voices from deep in my subconscious—they have to be wrong. I have to be wrong when

I think there's something weird going on with them.

It's impossible. I'm being paranoid. This life is just making me totally paranoid, and I'm letting the fact that my dad is missing throw all my instincts off. This is textbook psychological crap: I can't figure out the answer I need, so I'm finding bad guys everywhere.

Get a grip, Gaia.

Natasha—I mean, okay, she's not being as active in her investigation as I think she should be. That doesn't mean she's double crossing me and my dad. Or that she's somehow behind his disappearance. That's just crazy!

And so what if Tatiana ratted out Sam and me to Ed—that's more about her being so desperately in love with Ed, right?

Ugh.

I'm trying to believe my own pep talk. But these weird little details keep popping up, and I feel like pieces of a jigsaw puzzle are putting themselves

together, and I hate the picture
that's starting to appear.

   If Natasha and Tatiana turn
out to be bad. . . I don't know
what I'll do. I don't think I'll
ever be able to trust anyone,
ever again. Not even Dad.

   Not even myself.

Interesting. Very

interesting. Apparently the word
cannoli has secret powers I would
never have predicted. Apparently
it can make a tall blond high
school girl vanish without a
trace. Maybe I should notify
someone.

Like who? Most people would
like to make a statuesque blond
appear, not disappear.

I'm the only one trying to get
the hell away from one. From the
moment I met Gaia, my world has
been a constant chaotic mess. My
feelings have gotten twisted, wrung
out, and stomped on. My friends
have gotten hurt. I've gotten hurt.
I really think the best thing is to
keep away from her and clear my
head. I need some space.

But I feel really bad. . . .
It's not like I want to hurt her
feelings. And that's just what I
did. That talk could not have gone
worse. I was just trying to say,
Come on, Gaia, you can act this
way, you can make me feel like I'm

wanted if you really try. If I *am* really wanted. But every time I opened my mouth, jeez, the wrong thing kept coming out. I felt like Adam Sandler. The eternal schmuck. I think I made her think I'm going to start dating Tatiana. That the things Tatiana does for me make me like her.

I mean, they do. I do like Tatiana, but I don't LIKE her, like her. Not the way I like Gaia. I—I mean, I love Gaia. Even if I can't be her boyfriend—even if I can't really trust her—I'm always going to care about her.

And if she ever decided to start treating me the way Tatiana does? I think I'd forgive her for everything.

But I guess that's one of the raving ironies of this world. Someone you kind of like treats you like the king of hearts, while the one you'd lie down and die for treats you like the joker.

Guess I'm not going to get what I want in this hand. I'm not even sure what I want, anyway, so it's just as well. But no matter what, the cards are stacked against me.

Royal flush. Bad deal. Go fish. Insert bad playing-card metaphor here, indicating that Ed Fargo is one confused dude.

Whatever. I fold. Gaia Moore, you're too rich for my blood.

If she
could
prove
herself
wrong,
she'd be
really,
really
happy.

oh.
shit.

A FEW MINUTES AFTER GAIA LEFT

The Suckiest

Natasha poked her head into the room and caught Ed in a complete zone-out, staring at the wall, inwardly muttering about Gaia.

"Ed," she said.

He looked up with a start. "Oh, sorry," he said. "I'm all done here."

"I know she has not been kind to you," Natasha said, stepping into the room and leaning against the doorjamb.

"Tatiana's great."

"I mean Gaia. I am afraid I heard your conversation, and I know she is not being easy to get along with."

"Oh. That's Gaia, I guess," he said. "It's no big deal. We were friends for a long time; that's the only thing that's a drag about it."

"Well, I want you to know that I think you are a very nice boy, and if she cannot see that, then you are better off with someone else."

Ed felt his face flush with confusion. This was a speech he might expect from his own mom—if his mom was the mom from *Seventh Heaven*—but from Gaia's own almost stepmother? It seemed weird. Then again, Gaia was weird, too. Maybe Natasha just wanted her daughter to be dating him, the Nice Guy. That was a nauseating thought.

"Well, thanks," he said.

"I am glad you and Tatiana are friends," she said.

"Forget about your troubles and try to have a good time, okay? You are young; you shouldn't be tied up in knots and talking to a wall."

Ed laughed. "You weren't supposed to see that," he said.

"Do not worry. I have a houseplant that could collect a fee for being my therapist. I am going out now—don't feel that you have to run out. Finish what you are doing. And I will see you later, Ed."

Ed nodded, and Natasha left the room and the apartment. The silence of the big old place hummed in his ears. Turning back to the computer, he noticed that the last CD was finished. He slowly unhooked all the wires and packed away his equipment.

On the way downtown in the subway Ed cycled through the songs on his MP3 player, watching idly as the titles flipped past his eyes on the little screen. Some of them were most definitely Gaia-and-Ed songs.

All right. Do I delete these? he wondered. *We're getting space, we're broken up, and I don't think we're getting back together. But if we do, I'll have to download them again, and that's a pain.* Ed felt like he could have used a handbook to help him figure out the rituals of breakups. When did a break become a breakup? Who deleted what, and when was the most acceptable time to do that? Ed was getting dizzy just thinking about it.

The more he thought about it, the more he wished he could transfer his feelings for Gaia over to Tatiana.

Just *fwoop!*—move them over there. Create a hybrid female who liked him the way Tatiana did and who made him feel comfortable and excited and interested all the time the way Gaia did. Minus all the drama and all the anxiety. Now that would be the perfect girl.

Too bad she was entirely fictional.

A wave of Gaia anger broke over Ed's head. He was so frustrated. She was being such a jerk: Why couldn't she just act like a regular person? In a frenzy he deleted every single song that had any connection to her at all, including any song that started with the letter *G*. Out. Gone. Delete. *Yes, I'm sure,* he told the little blue screen. The train rattled through the tunnel as he looked down at it.

Now he felt bad.

He wanted the songs back.

Breakups were the suckiest events ever invented. And this one had to be the suckiest in all of human history.

GAIA SAT ON HER PERCH ON THE

Nice Guy

roof of her building. Technically she wasn't supposed to be up here, but she wanted to cool off and think—and she wanted to get back into the apartment when it was empty so she could look around. She didn't like her new theory—that Natasha and Tatiana were involved in a plot to kill her—but she couldn't afford to stick her head in the sand. Not on this one. Besides, she was sure her theory was wrong—and if she could prove herself wrong, she'd be really, really happy.

Despite the clues she had put together, it was a fact: She wanted to believe in Natasha and Tatiana.

Being alone was just too hard. Always having to depend on herself was unfair. Most of the girls she went to school with couldn't commit to a pair of shoes without asking the opinions of at least twenty people. Why did she have to make major life-and-death decisions with no help?

She watched Natasha exit the building, wearing a long red coat. Her white legs in high black pumps stood out against the dull concrete. Her dark hair tumbled down her back, so shiny Gaia could admire it from ten stories up. She looked like a perfume ad. Gaia could see why Tom loved her. She ached for her father, feeling his absence like a heavy, itchy army blanket.

A few minutes later Ed trudged out the front door, walking the same path Natasha had, toward the subway. He carried his skateboard loosely under one arm. Gaia squelched the pang she felt for him. Or tried to, anyway.

The apartment was empty; that was the important

thing. She went back inside the building and let herself into the silent rooms. She'd been living here for weeks and had made it her business to look over the whole place the minute she'd moved in. She hadn't found anything suspicious or incriminating back then. But this time she had much more serious evidence against them.

She could only hope it was false evidence.

TATIANA WAS PLAYING INTRAMURAL

Body racquetball, and Ed wanted to catch her performance. Since their high school didn't have a court, Ed joined a throng of students at a nearby gym. It was a gym designed especially for the tragically hip, and it looked like a disco. It even had a name—Smash. He passed the aerobics studio on the way downstairs—or tried to, anyway. Suddenly Ed understood why racquetball was drawing such a healthy crowd, especially of male students. The aerobics studio had tall silver poles in it, and women in workout gear were climbing up and down them, writhing like oversexed snakes as club music pounded and purple lights flashed around the room. He eyeballed the sign: Strip-aerobics. Clearly the VS administration had neglected to check out the Smash class schedules.

"Nice," he said.

"I love our school," a redheaded freshman kid stated with complete conviction. "It's worth every penny my parents pay."

"Come on, stud," Ed said, clamping a hand on the kid's shoulder and walking him down the hallway toward the racquetball courts.

"Oh, man," the kid groaned. "Just five more minutes?"

"I think you've seen enough to keep you going till your prom," Ed told him. "Anyway, if you time it right, you can leave during hip-hop class."

"I am so glad I didn't get into Stuyvesant."

Downstairs, students stood on the benches and sat on the floor to get the best view of the glassed-in racquetball court. Inside, Tatiana was fighting her third opponent of the day. Her stamina was unbelievable. So was her muscular body. Ed didn't like to think of himself as someone who objectified women, but looking at Tatiana clad only in a tank top–sports bra and bike shorts, he had to give in to his inner red-blooded American male. Her hair was pulled back in a sleek ponytail, and even her eye-protection goggles looked hot. But really, the most amazing thing about her was the determination and focus she displayed on the court.

Spinning her racquet, glaring at the ball, and springing into action when her opponent slammed the little blue orb against one of the white walls,

Tatiana was like a superhuman sportsbot, leaping around the cube-shaped room at a speed that made everything else look like slow motion. She managed to anticipate the angles the ball would travel along and a few times seemed to hit it without even looking toward it. Everyone broke into applause when she actually ran up the wall and flipped backward to make a shot. Nobody had a chance against Tatiana.

Ed was amazed. He'd known Tatiana had athletic ability, but he'd had no idea she was such a monster. Something about her seemed oddly familiar to him. She was so strong, powerful, focused, she was almost like. . . *Gaia! Ack!*

Tatiana's got nothing to do with Gaia, Ed told himself. *You just happen to like strong women—you're not attracted to Tatiana just because she reminds you of Gaia.*

Wait a minute. Attracted?

Before he could question that little voice inside him about what, exactly, it meant by "attracted," Tatiana won her last match and exited the court to more cheers and whistles. She was greeted by a gaggle of girlfriends and had to give a dozen high fives to admiring students. But the minute she pulled her goggles up on top of her head, her eyes searched out Ed. She came across the room to him, laughing and wiping the sweat off her face with a white towel.

"You won!" he told her.

"It looks that way. Would you like a hug?"

"Absolutely not!"

Tatiana gave a breathless laugh. "I am going to take a shower. After that, would you come and eat a giant mountain of pasta with me?"

"Sure, good plan," Ed said. "And I've got your CDs."

"How did I get so lucky? You are a good pal," she told him before she vanished into the locker room.

I am a good pal, Ed told himself. *A good pal. See? She's over that trying-to-kiss-you phase.* He was relieved to be out of the potential boyfriend slot. His feelings over Gaia were still too jumbled to add a new love interest to the mix. He wanted to just hang out, enjoy the attention, and fill the time he used to spend with Gaia.

Tatiana joined him in front of Smash in record time, freshly showered and dressed in jeans and a sweater. Ed watched as she inspected her cell phone for messages—then inspected a second one, too.

"What's with the two phones?" He laughed. "You need one for each ear or what?"

"Oh—one is my mom's," she explained quickly. "We were shopping and she left it in my bag by accident, and I just can't help seeing who might be calling her. Aren't I a terrible daughter?"

The story tumbled out in a rush, almost as if she had thought it through carefully in case anyone asked. Ed thought that was kind of weird. But it didn't really warrant thinking about. Especially when she looked up and gave him a dazzling smile of the you're-the-only-person-on-earth variety. That pretty much wiped any question from his mind. Stuck on Gaia or not, he liked being in the company of this very pretty girl.

"Okay, how did you get ready so fast?" he asked. "It takes my sister half an hour just to brush her hair. And that's right after she's had it blow-dried at the salon."

"I am magical," she said, hooking an arm into his. "And I am also starving."

"We can to go to Cucina in the East Village," Ed told her. "They serve the food on platters the size of flatbed trucks. If you can finish what's on your plate, I'll be seriously impressed."

"I think I will finish my food and yours," Tatiana told him. "Now tell me, did you run into Gaia when you were at my apartment, or were you safe from her prickly words?"

"No, she showed up," he said. "It was weird. She thinks something's going on between you and me." *If Tatiana's really taken me out of the potential boyfriend slot, she'll think that's funny,* Ed thought.

"Oh. Really?" Tatiana asked, peering at the cracks in the sidewalk.

Oops. Damn. Time to clarify things, Fargo.

"Yeah. She was asking how close we are, and I was trying to tell her that we're just really good friends, so I pointed out the cannolis and the bobble-head dog you got me and she just, like, left."

133

"She left?"

"Yeah. She looked at the bag and muttered something about Eleventh Street and Chinatown, and when I looked up, she'd left the room."

Tatiana didn't say anything. Her arm was still hooked through Ed's, but her hand gripped his anxiously as her steps slowed and she stared off into space.

Ed felt a sinking feeling of déjà vu. Walking down the street with a girl who seemed completely occupied with a mysterious, secret question. For the second time that day Tatiana was acting like Gaia.

"Tatiana?" he said.

"Yes," she said. "Oh! I am sorry, Ed. I just remembered something, but I can take care of it tomorrow."

"Did you leave something at the gym? Want to go back?"

"No, it is nothing. I just realized that I might have been careless with some. . . I might have done something careless. But it is nothing I cannot put right." She shot him a cheerful smile, erasing the Gaia scowl he thought he'd seen on her face.

"You're sure?" he asked, hoping she wouldn't excuse herself and leave.

"I am positive! In fact, I am thinking maybe we should have Indian food instead of Italian. Would you like that, Ed?"

"I could go either way," he said. "As long as we're eating."

"Oh, we are eating, my friend." She giggled. "We are having an eating contest."

They walked together through the city as the air thickened into night around them, scrolling through purple to black as they moved across town. By the time the sun was gone and their vegetable samosas hit the table, Ed was feeling fine. Tatiana was cheerful, funny, and carefree. She was nothing like Gaia. Nothing, nothing at all. Ed had found himself a Gaia-free zone, and that was just what he needed to stop missing her. Maybe even to get her out of his mind entirely. For now, anyway. Gaia-free for a night. That's what he needed to be.

GAIA CLOSED THE DRAPES AS THE SKY

Evil Ice

outside darkened into evening. During the day she couldn't be seen through the window, but since she had to turn on the lights, anyone peeking in would be able to plainly see her systematic inspection of every inch of the apartment. It wasn't likely that someone would do such a thing. But unlikely things were pretty much central to her life, and she wasn't about to take any chances.

She had dismantled and reassembled almost every

135

room in the house, finally arriving at the bedroom she and Tatiana shared. So far she had found nothing but a lot of dust bunnies, three buttons, and $5.32 in change. Proof of nothing but some lax housekeeping. Hardly the kind of indictment she both dreaded and was searching for.

This room, though. Where could something be hidden here? After checking all the furniture for false bottoms and compartments, she moved to the walls, knocking on each bit of plaster to listen for a hollow sound, something that might indicate the presence of a safe.

There was nothing.

She inspected the floorboards next. Any looseness, any variation in color—all of it was suspect. Again her search turned up nothing. She gritted her teeth, frustrated. She refused to feel relieved. She sat with her back against the wall, glaring across the room at the old, nonworking fireplace. The hole in the middle of it seemed to stare back at her like a big, blank eye. A big, blank eye that went nowhere and. . .

Oh. Shit.

The fireplace.

Gaia sprang from her seat and inspected the marble structure. This was a standard feature of New York apartments—an ancient chimney that had been closed off when the building got steam heat. A lot of people kept the structure of the fireplace with a false front just because it looked nice. Some even went so far as to put a gas burner in there, with faux logs that glowed like a real fire. This one was just a piece of metal. A piece of heavy, decorated iron that moved with a deep, heavy sigh when Gaia pulled at it. She yanked it away from the wall and saw that a compartment had been built into the old chimney.

Well, that certainly went against city regulations.

So did the object in the hole.

A high-powered rifle. Sniper style.

Gaia sat back on her butt with a thump, staring at the firearm with heart-sinking resignation. She could hear the bullets flashing past her ears. Could feel their heat as they barely missed her head. She'd studied firearms technology. She'd even grabbed a shell casing from the Ukranian church. She pulled it out of her pocket now and held it next to the rifle, a nasty-looking bit of machinery that would probably feel more at home in a South American cartel than here on the Upper East Side.

Perfect match.

Without pausing to listen to the wailing in her heart, Gaia stood, replaced the metal, and gathered her essentials: some clothes and. . . well, that was it. She was used to traveling light. It all went into her messenger bag and she was out the door like a shot. She felt violated, disgusted, like she was crawling with mites. Like it had rained maggots on her. Like she'd been living in a pit of snakes. Beautiful, friendly snakes.

She had known that she couldn't trust Tatiana and Natasha, but she had done it, anyway.

She'd been off her guard for weeks, sharing a bedroom with a cold-blooded killer.

She had accused Sam of being the one after her—and now his injured expression was burned in her memory as that of a totally innocent bystander. Sam, who'd taken bullets and survived weeks and weeks of imprisonment without knowing why. And she'd turned on him.

She had left Ed, her buddy and her boyfriend, in the company of a rancid chick with evil ice in her veins. And no matter how much she wanted to warn him to stay away from her, she knew—after the way they'd been nonspeaking to each other—that he'd never believe it. He'd think it was petty jealousy, not pure protectiveness.

And worst of all, she had let Natasha and Tatiana into her heart. She'd given them something she never gave anyone: her respect and her trust. Knowing she had been so wrong made her feel like there was nothing beneath her feet but miles of blue sky.

Gaia Moore had really screwed up this time. But she couldn't do anything until she was sure of what she was doing. So far, since her father's disappearance, Gaia had been flying by the seat of her pants, stomping around the city and having temper tantrums, bouncing from one neighborhood to the next, having weird chance encounters that seemed to lead her somewhere and just turned her in circles again.

She had to get rid of this gun. And then she had to leave the city for a while. Natasha and Tatiana were sure to know, or at least suspect, that she had found the gun. And they'd know she knew the truth about them.

Oh God. Oh *God*! The truth about them! That this home that she'd made was fake, that every word they'd ever spoken to her was a lie! Gaia felt her throat tighten all over again. Her mind dipped dizzily into fury and sorrow.

It was impossible to think with all these feelings swirling around. She had to get out of there. She grabbed the gun, shoved it into her bag, and left as quickly as she could. The door slammed behind her with a thud that echoed a thousand times in her head. She wouldn't be back. From now on she had nowhere to stay.

Gaia had to get a grip. Find a way to focus and set out a plan. And to do that, she had to leave her own contaminated turf and lose herself somewhere else for a while. Anywhere, as long as it was far away.

It was like
Great
Adventure
after a
nuclear
apocalypse.

too

much

fun

THE TRAIN OUT TO BROOKLYN WAS

Cardboard Skeletons

almost empty. It was a great place to sit and think. Like having her own private office, Gaia thought, except it wasn't really private and most places of business didn't have floors covered in pee.

But the comforting rumble of the train as it took her downtown was soothing. She propped her feet up on the seat next to her and watched people get on and off.

Different stops had different personalities. Midtown was for tourists and businesspeople; downtown was where hair got brighter and noses and eyebrows bloomed with piercings. But by the time the train shot out of the underground tunnels for its trip outside on the Manhattan Bridge, the crowd was a complete mix of every kind of person, from suit-wearing guys with briefcases to exhausted-looking women in fast-food restaurant uniforms. Manhattan from this distance looked like Emerald City, magical and simple and clean. The tall, glam buildings cleverly hid the trouble and confusion that existed just beneath the surface.

Gaia looked the other way, toward Brooklyn, and saw fewer tall buildings and lots of smaller neighborhoods. The girls she went to school with acted like the outer boroughs were no-man's-land, but Gaia thought that probably spoke well of the non-Manhattan sections of New York City. She had a sketchy knowledge of what was where. Brooklyn seemed like just the place to disappear for a while.

The crowd on the train thinned out as Gaia hurtled farther and farther from Manhattan. By the time she pulled into the last stop, Coney Island, Gaia was one of six people stepping out onto the outdoor platform, where the night air closed in around her. The entire station had been built with Astroland in mind—a permanent seaside carnival that hadn't been fancy since about 1907. It was like Great Adventure after a nuclear apocalypse: ancient, seedy, and busted up but charming and nostalgic at the same time.

Gaia walked through the amusement park. The fog that had closed in around her during the hour-and-a-half ride out of Manhattan—the haze of confusion, anger, and heartsick betrayal—began to lift just a little as she walked aimlessly around the park. She had to clear her head and figure out what to do next. Slowly she felt her consciousness begin to click into place, pushing her emotional miasma back into the box she had to keep it in, allowing Gaia to think clearly and logically.

As she looked around, she was amazed that anyone was there, but sure enough, a few families still straggled around the desolate rides. This place was a perma-holiday for the damned. An ancient roller coaster with wooden slats whipped people up and down a course of turns that Gaia thought couldn't be scarier than the 4 train at rush hour. The "haunted house" was a couple of dismal carts that rolled through a small structure decorated with truly terrifying cardboard skeletons. Go-karts buzzed around a figure-eight track, looking like they'd been constructed of leftover parts from a demolition derby. The place was like an old couch, one part comfy and two parts gross. Gaia loved it.

She stopped at a huge Ferris wheel that was the most obvious feature looming up out of the dark beachside neighborhood. Lights on the side of it spelled out *Wonder Wheel.* Gaia figured it was called that because everyone wondered why it didn't pop off its casters and roll over the boardwalk into the nearby surf. It had two kinds of cars: big white ones that sailed placidly in a neat circle and smaller ones in red, blue, and green that seemed just as placid until they got about halfway up. That was where they lurched sickeningly and rolled to the center of the wheel, sliding violently back and forth before speeding back out to the outer edge of the wheel. Those cars really looked like they wanted to pop off and sail over into the carousel. Gaia could hear thin, high screams drifting down from the lurching cars. They did the same thing on the way down; when they came back around to the entrance, the doors to one of them opened, revealing a small family in a hurry to get out.

The mom and dad of the family getting out of the

Wonder Wheel were laughing, and a big brother looked a little embarrassed as a girl, about ten years old, wailed at the top of her lungs. She was shaking as her mother put her arms around her, stroking her wavy brown hair and trying to shush her.

"She'll be okay," the operator told them, and the mom said, "I know."

The dad leaned down and spoke to the girl. "LuAnne, look, you don't have to be scared," he said. "You're safe on the wheel; it just feels scary, but you're okay."

"I don't like that ride," the girl wailed.

"Come on, it's not scary," her older brother insisted, waving a hand derisively.

"Don't let him fool you—he cried, too, the first time he went up," the mom said. The little girl looked up at her, amazed. "Ask him," the man said.

"You got scared?" the girl asked her brother. He rolled his eyes, stood back for a moment, and then laughed.

"Yeah, I was scared," he admitted, and his sister laughed, too. He pulled her back a bit and pointed to the huge wheel stretching above them in the sky. "This thing has been up there for like a hundred years," he told her. "Look at how they made it—those things never fall off. It's strong, see? It feels bad, but you're safe in there. Probably safer than when *Papi's* driving."

"Hey," the dad growled. The girl looked dubious.

"I don't like the way it feels," she said.

"That's 'cause you're a wuss," her brother told her, and she gave him a punch and started chasing him through the park, away from their parents, who yelled at them to slow down as they strolled to the next ride.

Something about the scene made Gaia feel like her stomach was made of lead. Was she pissed at the parents for taking the kid on the ride? No. Gaia realized she was sick with envy. Jealous of a child who'd thought her world had spun out of control but then found out everything was okay—because her family wouldn't let her get into anything really dangerous.

As opposed to me, Gaia thought. *In my case, there's no safety inspector making sure I'm rolling on my track. No one to catch me when I fall. In fact, there are monkeys loosening the bolts on my car, and when I feel like I'm falling, I really am.*

It was enough to make a girl need some cotton candy.

Gaia bought a bag of pink flax and broke off a piece, letting it melt in her mouth as she walked slowly out of the park and onto the boardwalk. A long pier stretched out into the darkness, lights twinkling at the end of it, just barely visible.

She walked all the way down. Here the wind was stronger, colder. She hunched her shoulders, feeling almost like she could be blown into the black waves at any moment. When she got to the end, she leaned against the wooden railing and pulled the rifle out of her bag, one handed. Never even put down her cotton candy. She saw the metal glint for just a second in the moonlight, then dropped it unceremoniously into the deep, cold, salty water.

She didn't look at it, didn't make a snappy comment about a watery grave, didn't even pause to reflect on the fact that it had almost been the agent of her death.

It was gone, and that was that.

There's only one thing to do, she thought as she gazed down into the inky blackness below her. *I've got to watch my own back. Check my own bolts. Run my own Ferris wheel. I've been doing it since I was twelve. Just because I thought for a moment that I didn't have to anymore doesn't mean I can't learn to do it again.*

She followed the pier back down to the boardwalk and turned right, walking along the strip of boardwalk between the beach and the amusement park, toward the tall towers of the residential buildings of Brighton Beach. After ten minutes she was totally out of range of the bright lights and well into dangerous territory. But she wasn't too worried. She could take care of herself. Unlike most people.

Unlike the woman wrestling with a couple of muggers about fifty yards away.

What kind of woman in her right mind would walk this boardwalk alone at night? Gaia wondered. A homeless person, maybe. Someone from out of town or someone who was lost. But now was not the time for profiling.

Gaia dropped her cotton candy and thundered down the boardwalk toward the attack in progress. The most likely result would be that the bullies would want to avoid any kind of confrontation and would drop their task and run at the first sign of interference. But Gaia kind of hoped they wouldn't do that. She could use a good ass-kicking right now. Anger still whirled in her head, and this could be just the stress-reducing workout she needed.

Yahoo! The muggers didn't even acknowledge her approach. An ass-kicking was just what was required. And Gaia was ready for it. She kicked forward, hard, making contact with someone's chest. The two guys dropped the woman, who ran shrieking toward the lights of the tall projects at the end of the boardwalk. Now it was just Gaia and her new friends. Fists rained on her from either side, and the second guy grabbed her from behind, an arm across her windpipe, trying to cut off her air supply.

Gaia grabbed at the arm across her throat instinctively, then put her training into action, turning her head to the side and shoving briskly upward with her hands. Your average girl would have had no effect on the oversized arm encircling Gaia's throat. But your average girl was not Gaia Moore.

Her choke-hold attacker fell forward, then grabbed at the air in confusion as Gaia stepped back and took a fighting stance. She gave a whirling roundhouse kick that caught one of the guys in the nuts; he tried to grab at her foot, but it was obvious that his only training was as a street fighter, and he was too uncoordinated to disable her. She shoved the heel of her hand into his face and felt his nose break, blinding him with blood and tears. She didn't know how many other guys were on the shadowy dark boardwalk with her and didn't want to stick around to find out; Gaia took off running, sprinting down the boardwalk toward a streetlight, hoping there would be an exit back to the street there. She wasn't sure how many of these guys she could disable before they overpowered her.

Behind her she heard their footsteps thundering and realized she had really pissed someone off. She'd robbed these guys of an easy mark, and now they wanted revenge.

Gaia needed to turn the tables. Stepping into an alley, she leapt up onto a fire escape and waited a moment. She heard their footsteps approach and leapt quickly down with her full weight onto the last of the goons—there were three now, she could see that—and punched at his face from above. Gaia had both gravity and surprise on her side. The guy tumbled to the sidewalk and gave a shocked yell as she stomped her foot on his face. The other two stopped to look back. In that brief moment under the streetlight Gaia could see the damage she'd done to one of their noses. She gave a battle yell and ran at them like a crazy person, swinging a crowbar she'd found on the fire escape. She felt a thud as it made contact with some part of one of the two guys; that was all they needed. She almost laughed as she saw them start running again—in the opposite direction.

Now she had a taste for the fight. Though she knew logically she should quit while she was ahead, some ancient, instinctive voice from the deep recesses of her brain told her she was having too much fun. Her legs agreed and took off after them, racing to catch up and cause more damage. Attack a defenseless little female on the boardwalk, would they? She'd show them. Anger pumped through her veins along with adrenaline to keep her going at top speed.

But the goons knew this neighborhood, and she didn't. As they approached an avenue, they split off in two different directions. Gaia looked wildly up and down, through the sparsely populated street under the elevated train. One man hopped into a sedan that sped off; the other crossed in front of a bus and disappeared down a side street. She tried to run after that one, but a bus lurched in front of her, stopping her with a deafening honk as she felt the warm air of its exhaust hit her in the face. By the time it passed, the guy had melted into the night. Gaia's chase was over.

She stood for a long moment. She knew what would come next. After any ass-kicking there was a price to pay, and it came upon her from behind now with the force of an explosion: total exhaustion, turning her limbs to rubber and her guts to lead. She heard it in her ears, saw the world fade to black, and felt her back hit the sidewalk as she tumbled to the ground, unconscious.

HER EYES OPENED AND GAIA SAW. . .

uh. . . what?

Lights. Tons and tons of lights. Gold frescoes in arches. And a bear. A huge brown bear wearing a leather harness and standing in a ring of people. What the hell?

Carb— Loaded Coma

Her vision cleared a little. The bear was nothing but acrylic paint. Part of a mural on a vaulted ceiling. She blinked twice and faces came into view, ringed around the edge of her vision and looking down at her with varying expressions of worry, concern, and bemusement.

"She's awake!" someone said, and several voices gave a cheer.

Gaia tried to sit, and a soft pair of hands helped pull her up.

"You're passing out in front of my restaurant!" The hands and the voice belonged to a stout woman wearing heavy sky blue eye shadow under short, bleached blond hair.

"I'm so sorry," Gaia said. "I'll go."

"Seeet!" the woman said, shoving Gaia right back down. Her arms were the size of huge legs of lamb, and their slack skin quivered as she sat Gaia on a high stool with surprising strength. "You are drunk?" she asked suspiciously.

"No," Gaia said. The woman smelled her breath, seemed satisfied, and clapped.

"Then you are hungry," she announced. She rattled off a series of orders in Russian and slapped the bar next to Gaia.

Gaia looked around her. This place looked like a palace—well, kind of. A palace built of plastic and mirrors instead of stone and tapestry. Everything around Gaia was shiny, reflective, and marbled. The bar stools were tall chairs with white pleather seats and shiny gold backs; the bar was cool black Formica with a gold pattern of flecks and veins twisting through it. Behind it, bottles gleamed in front of a mirror that wrapped all the way around an already huge room, making this restaurant look like a vast cavern of festive tables. Wherever she was, Gaia had a feeling there was a party here nightly.

"My name is Luda," the woman told her. "You?"

"Gaia," she told her. The woman's forehead wrinkled in dismay. "Guy-a," she repeated.

151

Luda shrugged and squeezed Gaia's knee. The man behind the bar, a huge bear of a man who looked as big as the creature in the mural over their heads, said, "You need strength. Good vodka wake you up, make you feel powerful."

"No, no, that's all right," Gaia told him.

"Don' be stupid," Luda yelled, smacking the man on his huge forearm with a resounding slap. "She needs food." As if on cue, three heaping plates of food rattled onto the counter, brought by a beefy man in a stained apron holding a cigar in the corner of his mouth.

"Stuffed cabbage," Luda told her, pronouncing it "*cebbedge*," the way Natasha and Tatiana did. For a moment Gaia felt a cold shudder run through her. Were these people friends of her newest enemies? Was she about to be ambushed? But as she looked around the room, she saw nothing to make her feel nervous or suspicious. Besides, Natasha was so tasteful and vain; she'd never be caught dead in a place this tacky. Gaia relaxed as much as she ever did and tried a piece of the cabbage.

It was rich and flavorful—one cabbage roll felt like it could satisfy her for a month. And it just kept coming: bow-tie pasta with barley in a thick gravy, blintzes buried in thick sour cream. . . the kind of food that was designed to get you through a cold Russian winter.

A distant memory flamed up in Gaia's consciousness. Her mother. A fragrant kitchen. Snow outside but bright, yellow warmth inside. And these flavors. This fantastic food, served by her mother. It made her want to sob with the familiar comfort of it.

She couldn't believe how confused she felt. On the one hand, being here with these Russians reminded her of the way Natasha and Tatiana had tried to kill her. The horrible betrayal of it all. On the other hand, it brought back everything about her long gone, long dead mother—even the feel of her sweater against her skin, the warmth of her arms around a much younger Gaia. She had to get out of here. This outer-borough experience was making her feel confused and disoriented.

Gaia lost her appetite. She pushed her plate away, forcing herself to smile at Luda.

"That is delicious," she said. "Thank you."

"You eat more," Luda ordered. "You're skinny, like a stick. You pass out again if you don't finish food."

"I'm really okay," she said, standing up. "My parents will worry if I don't get home soon. How much do I owe you for the food?"

Luda waved off that ridiculous suggestion. "Where you going? I'll have Vahe drive you," she insisted. "He's got a Town Car."

"I'll get on the subway. It's really okay," Gaia said, giving her a hug. "You've already done too much—I'm embarrassed."

"You come back," Luda told her. "Come back and I feed you until you strong like me."

Gaia smiled and left the restaurant. God, what a homey place. Warm, safe, and caring. How come total strangers treated her like a queen and the people she'd been living with for weeks wanted her dead?

Just dumb luck, she supposed. She wished she could run back inside and eat brown bread slathered with thick butter until she went into a `carb-loaded coma`. But while she'd been sitting there, chowing down and making new friends, she'd realized how much she didn't belong there. While she was stuffing her face, her dad was suffering somewhere, and she was his only hope. And the only way she could find him was to spy on the spies she was living with.

The job seemed impossible. She dreaded the task ahead of her. But there was no other answer. She had to return to Seventy-second Street, act like she hadn't found anything out, and live in seeming ignorance, pretending to get along with Natasha and Tatiana while waiting for clues.

She had to climb back into the snake pit. `Sit among the snakes.` Let them slither over her. And listen for the secrets that their whispering hisses might reveal.

Putting the warmth of the restaurant behind her, Gaia faced the night chill and dragged herself reluctantly to the nearest subway.

ED SAT BACK AND LET OUT AN EXHAUSTED

Giggly

puff of air. "I don't think I've ever eaten that much in my life," he said, blinking helplessly at the exactly one mouthful of saag motor ponir sitting in the silver dish in front of him.

"I will take that," Tatiana said, scooping it up with her fork.

"That's unbelievable! Where are you putting it all, in your backpack?" he asked, peeking under the table to make sure she wasn't. "You know, a lot of girls are afraid to eat in front of guys."

"I am not a lot of girls," Tatiana said.

"Well, you eat like you're about seven of them."

"Hey, you guys!"

Ed looked up to see Megan and three other girls from school.

"Oh, you found us!" Tatiana cheered. "I didn't know if you got my message!"

"You left them a message?" The question just popped out of Ed's mouth. He hadn't meant to ask it. He was surprised to find himself feeling disappointed that he wouldn't have Tatiana all to himself. Despite all the times he had told her—and himself—that his romantic feelings were only for Gaia, he thought—this twinge of regret told him—he might have a little crush on Tatiana, too.

"Oh, did you think you were going to have her all

to yourself?" Megan cooed, as if she'd read his mind.

"No," Ed mumbled. This was an annoying development. He didn't want his feelings to get even more messy and jumbled. Besides, this was a boisterous bunch—even though there were only a few of them, they were so giggly and chatty that they filled the tiny, train-car-size restaurant with their presence. People at other tables kept glancing over. Megan's book bag boinked a lady sitting across the aisle.

"Well, we definitely need to adjourn to another location," Megan announced as the lady glared at her and tried to protect her food from any further unintended book bag onslaughts.

"Sounds good to me," Tatiana said. "We should go to Blue and Gold and play pool."

"Very badly? Can we play very badly?" Melanie begged.

"Well, you can," Megan told her. "I think I'm getting better at it. I'll kick your ass, anyway."

"I hope you don't mind," Tatiana whispered across the table as she gathered up her things.

"Of course I don't," Ed said. "I might go home, though."

"No! You have to come!" Tatiana grabbed his arm affectionately. "I want you to come, too. Please?"

Ed shrugged. The fact was, he was glad this giggly posse had shown up. They'd stop another awkward confrontation from happening—like when Tatiana had tried to kiss him. If he was developing feelings for her, then he had to keep a comfortable distance. But he really wanted to be out. What was at home? Nothing but thoughts of Gaia.

"Okay, I'll come." He nodded. They went to the divey bar a block away and took over the back room, writing their names on the little blackboard so their mini–pool tournament could proceed. Then the girls started knocking the balls around on the green felt. They clearly had no clue how to play.

Ed couldn't resist. "You might want to hold it like this," he told Megan. "Look, between your knuckles so the cue actually goes where you're aiming it. Hit this one over here," he added, pointing out the sweet spot on the seven ball.

"Ohmigod, it went in!" Megan yelped. "Yay, I'm a pool player!"

Soon he was giving a miniclinic to the assembled girls. "This should have been your intramural activity, not skateboarding," Tatiana teased.

"You're probably right," he said. "Especially since there's a definite irony in my teaching skateboarding after what I did to myself. I should have handed out wheelchairs to everyone who took it."

Tatiana laughed. "Ed, you're terrible!" she scolded.

Someone handed him a Sam Adams, and Ed took it. It was fun playing pool, but if he'd been given his choice of activities this evening, hanging out with these girls would not have been one of them. As the novelty of the pool lesson wore off, there was more chatting and less ball-hitting. Ed noticed there was a distinctly catty turn to the conversation.

"I mean, I don't know who told her Burberry was still in style, but she was wearing that pukey plaid with no shame whatsoever."

"Wait, maybe she was being funny."

"No, she was not. She was just wearing it. I don't know why she didn't pair the skirt with a pair of Y2K commemorative sunglasses and some dot-com stocks. She looked so ninth grade."

"Maybe tomorrow she will wear the Ralph Lauren puppy sweater," Tatiana added to the conversation, pronouncing Ralph Lauren with the correct non-French accent and indicating not only a knowledge of but an interest in both fashion and bitchery. Ed wilted slightly. This wasn't a surprise, but it was a side of Tatiana that wasn't his favorite.

"I heard her father lost a bundle on that merger that never happened," someone else added. "But if she's scrounging, she's better off wearing no name than old names."

"She's better off staying home if she's going to let her ass get that big," Tatiana said. "Did anyone notice that the stripes looked like ocean waves?"

Everybody busted up laughing. Ed had no idea who they were talking about, but something about the conversation was making him kind of sick. Yeah, it was mean, but there was something else, too. He took a long swig of Sam Adams and suddenly felt dismally tired. He put down his cue and went to sit on one of the banquettes.

I should be happy, he thought. *Here I am, out with the hottest girls in school, and I'm the only guy in sight. Isn't this like the plot of some teen movie? I should be having the time of my life.*

Woo-hoo. The trouble was, something about this scene—the bitchy girls, the fashion report cards, the endless chatter—was awfully familiar. Was he just having a random case of déjà vu or. . .

Ugh. He knew exactly what this reminded him of.

Way back in the far reaches of his memory, he had a vision of himself—young, nervous, and eager to impress his new girlfriend, Heather. He'd fallen for her because of the way she was when she was just with him. But a major flaw in their relationship was the way she became in these packs of females. He had spent too much time hanging out with her in places like this. Listening to her yak with her girlfriends. Struggling to keep up with their cleverer-than-thou bitchfests. Years later, after all he'd been through, he was ending up in the same circle of girls, doing the same shit. Only this time the queen bee was. . .

"Ed, don't be so mopey," Tatiana complained, coming over and yanking at his arm. "Everybody's having fun. What are you, a lightweight?"

Tatiana. She had somehow turned into the new Heather. And she wasn't the queen bee. She was acting like the queen bee-yotch. All of a sudden Ed felt like he'd been yanked back into Casa Heatherosa.

"I want to see someone doing a shot," she announced, like a demented cruise director. "Who is first?"

Maybe he was overreacting, Ed thought. Maybe Tatiana just had a couple of drinks in her and was acting obnoxious. But even if that were true, it made him like her less.

But that wasn't the worst part. The worst part was that this was the second time in twelve hours that Tatiana had reminded him of someone else. An ex-girlfriend, no less.

Am I so predictable that I'm going to spend the rest of my life dating the same two girls over and over again? he wondered. *Or is Tatiana somehow doing this on purpose?*

He had no idea which—if either—was true. He took a closer look at Tatiana. She had seemed like her old self when he went to her match, but now he was replaying it. There was something in her eyes, some kind of bitterness that hadn't been there before. Almost like she had experienced some great personal letdown, a betrayal so huge, it had changed her outlook on life.

But she hadn't said anything about having problems. They were friends, weren't they? Ed would have known if something huge had gone down. Maybe she was worried about applying to college? Ed's sister had

160

turned into an obsessed monster before she'd even ordered her applications, and every meeting with her adviser had thrown her into a deeper funk over how she'd never get into Bennington or Bard. Or something with her dad? Ed had never heard a full explanation of who he was or why he wasn't around. Most of his friends had an almost fetishistic interest in their absent parents. The more he thought about it, the more he realized something was off with Tatiana, and try as he might, he couldn't figure out what it could be. She did well in her classes, and she had tons of friends.

Oh, jeez, it's not me, is it? he wondered. *What if she's upset because she's hung up on me?* The idea seemed impossibly self-absorbed, but Ed couldn't dismiss it as a possibility. Given how messed up he'd been feeling over Gaia, he now had ample evidence that a sick heart could ruin every aspect of someone's life. And knowing he might be having that effect on Tatiana just made him feel even worse, and weirder, and less like a party animal. This night was getting really unfun.

Ed shook his head and took another swig of beer. It wasn't having the desired effect. His mind wasn't clearer, it was more clouded, and he was starting to feel like Heather, Gaia, and Tatiana were three freaky personality-switching sprites. Heather went from bitchy to nice. Gaia was so hot and cold, she was practically a split personality. And now Tatiana had gone from *Pleasantville* to *Cruel Intentions*.

Ed watched Tatiana from his spot on the banquette. This was just so confusing. The balls on the pool table made sense: You hit them and they rolled into each other. But Tatiana was one giant curveball, a cue ball that wiggled off in bizarre directions. Come to think of it, all girls were like crazy cue balls.

It was enough to make Ed seriously consider some sort of skateboarding monastery.

I think I have a few things pieced together. I know certain things. I know that I am Oliver Moore. I know that my brother, Tom, has a wife, Katia, and that I think about her more than I should. I still don't know who Gaia is. But she's somehow connected to my brother and. . . damn. Whenever I try to force my mind to tell me what that name means, I hit a brick wall of incomprehension. She's like a blind spot in my mind. Maybe she's my wife? Could I have a wife who I don't even remember? Gaia. No. I don't think she's my wife. It's more complicated than that. With time. With more time, perhaps I'll remember.

I still have no way out of my body. My eyes blink, my fingers will sometimes make spasmodic movements, but basically I am trapped in a flesh prison. It's like a diabolical form of torture. It's all I can do not to go mad, with nothing but the

nurses' gossip and the nattering
of daytime soap operas to fill my
head. I force myself into disci-
plined mind exercises. First,
when I was still very, very
bewildered, it was all I could do
to get through the multiplication
tables. I would recite them to
myself like a third grader learn-
ing them by rote all over again.
Then I found the numbers came
more easily. Like old friends. So
I moved on to the periodic table,
the elements. . . though something tells me there are a few
new ones that have been added
since I went into this vegetative
state. I try to remember sonnets
and speeches from Shakespeare.
Poetry is more difficult than
numbers, though. More variables.
Less logic. But my mind needs all
the challenges it can get.

Lord knows, my daily dose of
Family Feud will not stretch my
intellect at all.

Sometimes I lose hope. All
this thinking, all this repeti-
tion of memorization, and for

what? To lie here inside a body
that ignores me? Legs that lie
like far-flung lumps, arms that
splay out to his sides attached
by tubes to watery bags filled
with food and medication—I don't
blame the doctors for ignoring
me. I see them poke their heads
in, whenever they feel they
absolutely must, and they hurry
away as quickly as possible. They
must hate to be reminded that
they can do nothing about me.
They think I'm dead inside this
flesh; they'd like to fill me
with morphine and free up my
hospital bed.

Sometimes I feel so hopeless,
I wish they would. Sometimes I
wonder why I'm still alive if I'm
just going to lie here for the
next forty years. I just hope
that if my mind gets stronger, my
body will follow suit.

Six times twelve. The square
root of 6,561. Aluminum, boron,
and cadmium. "My mistress' eyes
are nothing like the sun." These
are the twisted helices that I

hope will help me evolve back into myself. If I can just hold on to my sanity long enough to get there. I'm Oliver Moore. I'm Oliver Moore, and I want to wake up. How long have I been like this? Am I getting better or just fooling myself? Why isn't my brother here?

Can't anyone hear me?

Nurse's Report, New York Hospital
2:30 A.M.

    Checked on patient Oliver Moore. No change in
demeanor or physical presentation of symptoms. No
response to queries or attempted stimulation.
Some movement of fingers. Determined to be random. Patient still assumed to be in a persistent
vegetative state.

And that
would be   **gun**
the end of
that.

AS SOON AS GAIA'S TRAIN HIT

Blushing Brick Red

Manhattan, she was struck with a sudden, urgent need to set things right with Sam. The thought was clear and crystallized in her mind, like a diamond on black velvet—either it was the adrenaline of the ass-kicking, the hearty food, or just getting away from it all that snapped her mind into focus. Or a combination of the three. Whatever the reason, Gaia was shocked and ashamed that she hadn't thought of it before. The gun in Tatiana's bedroom proved that Sam wasn't the shooter. Her suspicions of him had been totally unfounded. Whether or not she was unsure of her feelings for him—romantically, hormonally, or whatever—she'd been one billion percent wrong when she accused him of setting her up.

Tatiana might even have his cell phone now. It wasn't hidden with the gun, but Gaia had to assume, even if she wasn't one hundred percent sure, that either Natasha or Tatiana had sent her that text message.

Ugh! He had even told her the cell phone was lost, and she hadn't believed him! The memory of that washed over her in a whole new wave of shame that left her blushing brick red. Apologies weren't her strong suit, anyway; this one was making her squirm beyond belief.

Before she went home to play ignorant-innocent with Natasha and Tatiana—pumping them for information while she pretended she hadn't found the gun—she wanted to tell Sam how wrong she'd been. She replayed the scene from earlier in the day in her head. She saw Sam's surprise, his concern, and his hurt when she'd turned on him. Over and over again. It drove her up a wall. Okay, so given the information she'd had—that the text message had come from Sam's phone—she had been entirely justified in suspecting him. But she should have been able to weigh that evidence against what she knew about Sam: that he was the most soulful, kindhearted person she'd ever met and that unlike the embittered, world-weary people she usually had to deal with, he was incapable of hurting her. Gaia had been pissed at Ed for not trusting her—and that was exactly how Sam felt. She should have trusted him. She needed to say that to him, and she needed to do it now.

Never mind that she really didn't want to go back to Seventy-second Street. Never mind that she was hoping for something, anything, to make her feel good before she steeled herself for that snake pit. All that aside, she still wanted to apologize, and now was as good a time as any.

She got off the train downtown and ran east, from the chichi galleries of SoHo to the place where the Lower East Side met Chinatown. The t'ai chi park was empty now; nobody was out but a few homeless people and the occasional person obviously hurrying home to a family or friends. Gaia hoped there were friendly faces waiting for her, too.

She buzzed and was quickly let up. Dmitri answered the door. This time she wasn't in a huff over almost getting barbecued in a fire. She couldn't believe how much he had improved since they'd found him in the prison.

"Wow, you look great," she said. He did. Getting rid of his ratty long hair and putting food in his belly had given the old man a complete transformation. His blue eyes sparkled with intelligence.

"Did you find anything out about my dad?" she asked.

"Not yet, no," he said. "But I think you are not here to speak to me."

"No, I'm not. Is Sam around?"

"I'm right here," Sam said, and Gaia whirled around to face him. But now that she was here, she didn't know how to say anything.

"I wanted to—Dmitri, could we?"

"I'm going now," he said, padding off to the kitchen.

"I have to tell you something," she said to Sam, grabbing him by the arm and pulling him over to the window for the illusion of more privacy. As she looked at him, her heart gave a disconcerting little wobble. Here was the first guy she'd ever fallen in love with, the guy who'd made her see that there was more to the world than being pissed and playing chess in the park. He was thinner, more tired, badly injured. . . and all of it just made him look more handsome. Not in a movie-star way. In a real-person way. The way his brownish red hair fell onto his forehead, that same brown jacket that had hung in his NYU dorm room—she felt so much affection for him. She didn't know if it was like, or love, or what, but she didn't want this person to hurt because of her.

"I was horribly, horribly wrong this afternoon when I got mad at you," she said.

"Yeah." He wasn't being helpful.

"I'm serious," she said, grabbing his arm. "I accused you of setting me up. And it's not even like that was the first time I said something like that to you. I've been suspicious of you ever since you came back, and that must have felt horrible."

Sam shifted his weight and leaned against the wall behind him. He wasn't able to meet Gaia's eyes. "Yeah. It did," he admitted.

"Well, I found out some things today, and they all point to someone else setting me up—I know for a fact it was someone else. It wasn't you. I know that now, and I'm so, so sorry."

"You have proof?" Sam still wouldn't look at her. He was staring uncomfortably out the window, at the moon, just about anywhere but at Gaia. And the way he asked—he was almost sarcastic.

"Yeah. I found some pretty damning evidence."

"Well, I'm so glad that this *evidence* made you believe it wasn't me, Gaia." Sam sighed, finally turning his eyes to meet hers. They looked like sad brown puddles. "I just wish you had known that from the start."

"Sam, I'm sorry—I've had to watch my back for so long, it's just instinct," she tried to explain. "If you knew how many people have turned on me—"

"I know that," he said. "Look, I understand you're involved in something huge and weird. But it's turned you into someone I don't know how to deal with."

"I'm not asking you to deal with anything," Gaia said, finally putting a hand on his forearms, which were still crossed protectively across his chest. He didn't pull away—a tiny slice of relief. "I'm just trying to admit I was wrong and to apologize for the fact that you got caught in the cross fire," she went on, glancing down at his chest where his bullet wounds were still healing. "I'm not asking anything else from you."

As soon as she said the words, Gaia realized with a thud of her heart that it wasn't quite true. She might not be asking for more, but she *wanted* more. A lot more. Maybe not love and romance, but at least affection, friendship, a warm hug to get her through the next few days. Forgiveness. A friend.

"All right. Good." Sam stood, no longer leaning against the wall, and Gaia's hands dropped to her waist. She looked up at him helplessly. The ball was in his court.

"I understand what you're saying," he said. "I mean, I accept your apology. But I'm glad you're not asking anything else of me. I'm not sure I've got much left to give." His eyes flicked toward hers, but it seemed almost painful to him. He went back to studying the wooden slats of the floor. "We'll talk later, okay? I'll see you."

"Okay, bye," she said, though he had left the room by the time she got the words out. She felt like a total schmuck. And lonely. She felt weirdly lonely. She turned and saw Dmitri standing in the doorway.

"I'm sorry you had to overhear the latest episode of *Dawson's Creek*," she said.

"I am sorry you are having a difficult time with Sam," Dmitri said. "But perhaps you will feel better when I tell you what I have now found out."

"I have information, too," Gaia said. "It's horrible news. Because of it I may be killed if I go back to the apartment on Seventy-second Street."

"What?" Dmitri was incredulous. "Something about the women you live with? Natasha and. . ." His voice trailed off as he searched for the other name.

"Tatiana. Yes," Gaia said. "They're dangerous— more dangerous than I ever imagined. But if you can help me figure out how to handle them, we can get back to finding my dad."

She followed Dmitri into the kitchen. They both heard the front door of the apartment close with a slam. Sam was gone. Dmitri gave Gaia a sympathetic look. It wasn't much, but to her, it was the most affection she'd had in forever, and she accepted it gladly. She felt a wave of fondness for the old guy. Then she steeled her mind for the task ahead and sat down at the kitchen table to discuss what was going to happen next.

Okay, so that was everything
I wanted from Gaia. She admitted
that it was totally wrong to
accuse me and even agreed she
should have trusted me.

So why couldn't I do what I
wanted most? Why couldn't I gather
her up into my arms and give her a
crushing hug? She was so close, I
could feel the warmth of her body.
Her hands were on my arms. I was
so close, but something wouldn't
let me do it. . . .

I'm just angry. I'm really
still angry. I don't understand
how I could love someone so much
and she would still suspect me.
Of trying to kill her, for chrissake! It's such a deep, huge
thing to think I could do. She
just doesn't know me at all, and
that feels so weird.

I feel like now it's me who
can't trust Gaia. It was just so
crazy, the way she accused me,
the way she looked at me with so
much hate, with bullet-proof
glass in her eyes. There was

nothing I could do to get through
to her. No way I could make her
believe me. That was a cold, cold
feeling. It hurt like hell.

Gaia, I'm sorry. I wish I
could have reached out to you
like you were reaching out to me.
But it came a little too late for
the wholehearted response you
wanted. I have to test my heart
and see if it can still reach out
to you. If I still have the nerve
to get close to you. Whatever we
are to each other, it all has to
be on hold.

Sorry again.

Maybe tomorrow. Maybe someday.

But not now.

AT THE BAR ED WAS STRUGGLING TO

stay interested in the evening going on around him. He was planning to leave as soon as he could. The trouble was, every time he tried to make an excuse, Tatiana begged him to stay, and for some reason he wasn't telling her no.

Glowing Green Screen

What's going on here, Fargo? he asked himself. *Are you trying to make Gaia jealous? It's not like she's here to see this. Or are you seriously whipped—by a girl who's not even your girlfriend?*

He was sitting next to Tatiana when she reached into her pocketbook and pulled out a strange cell phone. It wasn't the one she'd been using that morning. She studied it as if she were checking for an incoming call she might have missed, then put it back in her bag. Ed remembered the two cell phones she'd pulled out after her racquetball game. Now it struck him as weird all over again.

"What is with that thing?" he asked. "You've been checking it all night."

"It's a cell phone, silly."

"Yeah, but it's your mom's cell phone."

"So?"

"So why are you so worried about it?"

Tatiana turned to him, turning up the heat in her

eyes with a teasing wink. "Oh my, so many questions," she said. "Do you really want to know what is going on with my mother's messages?"

"No!" Ed gave an I-surrender wave. "Forget I asked. Whatever."

"Such an inquisition," Tatiana went on. "For someone who says he wants to be just friends, you do show an unusual amount of interest."

"Jeez, Tatiana," he began, but he was cut off by a strange ring. It was the mysterious cell phone. Tatiana took it out of her bag and stared at the glowing green screen.

"Aren't you going to answer it?"

She didn't even answer. Just stared at the ringing phone for three. . . four. . . five. . . six rings, until it stopped. Then she waited, still staring, breathing slowly, until a small envelope popped up. It beeped once, announcing that there was a voice mail message. She put it back in her bag.

"I am exhausted," she announced to no one in particular. "I am getting in a cab and going home."

"Nooooo!" Megan said, hugging her like a long-lost relative. "You can't go!"

"I must go. I just realized what time it is. My mother is so angry about the party I threw, and if I am not home tonight, she will send me to one of those boot camps for unruly teens."

"That was a quick switch," Ed commented.

179

"Oh, look who is trying to tempt me to stay out," Tatiana sang, totally missing (or pretending to miss) Ed's jab. First she'd begged him to stay out—and now that he'd stayed, she was making her exit faster than Cinderella at 11:59? It didn't make sense. But he didn't have a chance to ask her what was up. She was out the door before he could say a word, and by the time he got through the crush of girls between him and the door, she had slammed the door of her yellow cab. Through the window he could see her pull out the phone and hit one of the buttons to check the voice mail message. Then the cab sped away from the curb with a squeal, and she was gone.

He knew there were men who liked women with a little mystery. But right about now, Ed Fargo would have loved to meet someone ridiculously predictable.

Amazing. This apartment is completely empty of people. But full of whispers and ghosts, phantoms of the past, crowding me out of each room. I've been wandering from the kitchen to the living room to my bedroom, in search of peace each time but each time finding some new memory that pushed me away from comfort. Is it the apartment that's haunted? Or is it me?

It makes me laugh. Even when I make a home for myself, I am still a wandering nomad.

Look at this room, now. The room that is home to my daughter and Gaia. Tatiana was such a brilliant child. Even when she was tiny, running around on her sturdy legs and laughing in that charming, tinkling way that she had, I knew she was special. I watched her get what she wanted with charm and, when charm didn't work, with a well-placed chubby fist. I used to pretend to chide her, but underneath, I knew the two skills

would complement each other perfectly to take my daughter wherever she wanted in the world.

And I have done whatever I had
to do so that Tatiana could have
the most opportunities. Some very
distasteful things. And then,
some that were more pleasurable.
But it was all done for Tatiana.
So that she would never have to
live the way I lived.

Yet here, in the small twin
bed next to my precious daughter,
there has been an interloper.
Someone who wanted to usurp
Tatiana's birthright. I have been
forced to care for this ill-mannered creature, who did nothing
but resent me and spit in my face
in return for the care she was
given. And the worst part was, I
had actually begun to care for
this Gaia. For a brief period
things seemed calm, almost normal, almost homey.

Until I found out that this
mediocre child wanted the power
that Tatiana deserved.

That was entirely too much.

Just looking at their beds, you can see which belongs to the superior child. One, with fresh bedding neatly arranged, as pretty as a picture. The other, strewn with crumpled sheets, the pillow slumped on the floor like a defeated marshmallow. Who would live so disgustingly? The heiress to power? Or an annoying creature who must be eliminated?

Not many things really make me laugh. But there is no other response to this. To the idea that Gaia could ever be given such power when she so clearly doesn't deserve it. When power is exactly what Tatiana so richly deserves.

Not Gaia.

Tatiana.

And I will make that happen any way I can.

NATASHA FLUFFED HER DAUGHTER'S
pillow, stepped on Gaia's, and went over to
the false-backed fireplace to look at the gun.
She hoped to have an opportunity to use it
again soon. And this time she wouldn't
miss.

Gone

She moved the heavy piece of metal and peered
into the dim chamber, reaching for the instrument of
her revenge. Her hand closed on nothing.

Natasha gasped as if she had been bitten and
yanked her arm back out. She stepped back and looked
up at the wall, wildly thinking that maybe there were
two holes and she'd reached into the wrong one. But
there was just the one. It was supposed to hold the
beautiful gun. And it did not. It held nothing.

With a cry of fury she reached back into the dusty
chamber and flapped her arm desperately, trying to
locate the gun somewhere, anywhere inside. But all
she hit was bare walls and dirt. The gun was gone.

The gun was gone.

Had Tatiana taken it? Was she trying to act alone?
The thought hit Natasha like a cold fist clenching her
heart. Could she be so foolhardy? She would get herself
killed! She had picked up the phone to call her daughter when the real explanation blossomed in her mind.

Of course. It had to be.

Gaia had somehow found the gun and
taken it.

That little monster. Now Natasha wanted her dead more than ever.

The phone rang, startling Natasha from her reverie. She stepped into the kitchen and picked it up.

"She is going to Greenpoint. To the water towers near the docks."

It was Tatiana, sounding calm but excited. This was the chance they had both been waiting for. What they had failed at yesterday, they would now complete.

"My darling," Natasha said. "You're all right?"

"Of course. Why would you ask such a thing?"

"Just humor me," she said. "You don't have. . . anything you're not supposed to, do you?"

"What are you talking about? Of course not. Mother, are you all right?"

"It's nothing. Excuse me," Natasha said, relief flooding her veins. She composed herself quickly. "How did you find out about this odd location?"

"She called to tell Sam," Tatiana told her. She gave a lilting laugh. "She begged him to meet her—gave careful directions—said she had to be sure they would be alone. She says she has reason to be very paranoid. But she loves him and she must see him tonight."

"Oh, I'm sure she'll be just fine," Natasha said. "But we'll make sure, eh?"

"Do you know where these water towers are?"

"I will find out. You're coming home now?"

"I'm in the cab. I'm almost there."

"Good. By the time you get here, I'll be ready to go."

"I have to change. I'm dressed for a night out with those stupid girls."

"Yes."

Tatiana clicked off the line, and Natasha stood, holding the receiver as her daughter sped uptown toward her in a yellow cab. She caressed the telephone in her hand, as if her warm, loving hand would reach through to her daughter. No, Tatiana would never do something so foolish and ill-mannered. Only Gaia would take something that didn't belong to her. It made her dangerous, but now that Natasha knew where she would be, she'd be able to neutralize the troublesome girl, and that would be the end of that. It would be a little more difficult this way. She'd have to get close to her to end her life. But maybe that was the way it should be. Up close and personal. A final embrace for the girl who had almost been her stepdaughter.

She sat back in a plastic chair in the white-tiled kitchen. She was absolutely still. It was so quiet, she could hear the buzzing of the fluorescent light fixture above her head. She no longer felt the need to wander from room to room. Everything was ready to go. She simply waited for her daughter to come home.

A sharp
smell of
river
water **deserted**
pervaded
the air
out here.

NATASHA WAS GLAD SHE HAD USE OF the sleek black sedan that took her and her daughter across the Fifty-ninth Street Bridge. She found the red-and-white water towers easily— **Zagged** they were the only shapes rising out of the gloom of the warehouses surrounding them. A sharp smell of river water pervaded the air out here. And there was another scent: the scent of victory close at hand.

"So she is coming here to meet Sam," Natasha reiterated.

"Yes, I suppose she thinks this is a nice, romantic spot," Tatiana told her. "Yech."

"It is strange," Natasha said. "But she is such a strange girl. Nothing surprises me anymore."

"We should be careful. Maybe she will have the gun with her," Tatiana suggested.

"Not to meet her boyfriend. But of course you are right—we should always be careful, anyway." Natasha turned off her headlights for the final approach and put the car in neutral, slipping silently down the last block as they came within hearing range of the water towers. Then she pulled up the parking brake.

They were quiet for a moment. Both with an unspoken understanding that this moment of meditative silence would focus them for the task ahead. Full of anticipation, with a tiny bit of dread. But quiet and calm.

"Did you feel bad?" Tatiana asked.

"What?"

"Did you ever feel bad? About her father? And about her?"

Natasha turned to look at her daughter. So poised. So ready to take any action, with a maturity that set her completely apart from other girls her age. Yet Natasha could look into her eyes and see the pleading, unsure girl behind them. She took her hand.

"There are some sacrifices that must be made," she told Tatiana. "If it were easy, anyone would be able to do it. It is people like us, who have the bravery to make the difficult choices, who will always win. Remember, my *lapatchka*, we are soldiers first."

She was gratified to see the fear subside in Tatiana's eyes. But her gaze didn't waver.

"But you did not answer my question," she said.

Natasha looked away, out the windshield.

"Some sacrifices must be made," she repeated. "Now shush. Ready yourself. Tonight we must succeed."

Together she and Tatiana left the car and walked quietly out toward the looming towers. Everything seemed deserted, no sound but distant sirens and the quiet rustle of city life. In the bright moonlight they could see a figure with long blond hair standing uncertainly between the towers. Waiting for a boy who wasn't on his way. Because her phone call had come straight to Tatiana. It was too delicious.

189

The two women approached Gaia from two different directions, taking wide paths to the right and left of her so that they could complement each other's approaches and minimize the risk that she'd get away. From her vantage point Natasha couldn't even see Tatiana. But she could sense her presence, flitting like a bat in the dark shadows. When she was sure Tatiana was situated, she gave a loud whistle and began to run toward Gaia.

It was a bright night, and the open lot was lit by the moon. That was why they couldn't get too close without leaving the shadows. It meant Gaia had a good ten seconds before they could reach her. In that time she looked around, confused, and realized she was being ambushed. Quickly—so quickly Natasha almost had to admire it—Gaia turned and ran.

But she hadn't been expecting more than one attacker. She'd run away from the sound of the whistle and straight into Tatiana. Natasha's daughter clotheslined Gaia with a stiff-armed shot to the throat; Gaia ran right into the wrestling move and was knocked backward.

She stumbled, momentarily stunned, and then stepped backward a few paces. She zigged a few steps one way, then zagged in another direction, looking totally haphazard. This time it was Natasha who attacked her, grabbing her around the waist and slamming her into the metal wall of one of the water towers.

She heard the *thud* as Gaia hit the wall like a sack of wet sand. Then Tatiana arrived and grabbed her by the hair, snapping her head back and slamming it into the metal once, twice, three times in succession. Gaia let out little cries with each hit—but she didn't fall. Tatiana gave her one last angry shove and finally knocked her off balance. Gaia dropped to her knees and nearly fell to the ground, catching herself on her hands, instinctively pitching herself away from the two women.

"Wha—who—" she huffed. Natasha couldn't tell if she was asking or just gasping for air, but the damn girl was already running again, her feet moving one in front of the other as she flung her torso ahead of herself, doing an awkward, injured ballet in her effort to right herself.

Tatiana followed after her, grabbing for the waistband of her jeans. But Natasha could see Gaia twisting around, aiming a wild fist at Tatiana's head.

"No," she shouted, and Gaia turned, confused, before her fist could make contact.

"Natasha?" she asked. "What—what are you doing here?"

Damn. Cover blown. Oh well, it was bound to happen.

"Don't worry about why I'm here, Gaia," Natasha hissed. "Worry about whether you'll live long enough to leave."

"You found our little friend, eh?" Tatiana asked her. "Our third roommate. I wanted to use it to kill you. Now I have to find a different way."

"Oh my God—no," Gaia said. "Stay back. Stay away from me!"

This was too excellent. Natasha had never seen Gaia off balance before. The girl began running again, her blond hair looking blue as it flipped behind her in the moonlight, but Tatiana was right on her heels. Natasha saw her catch up to Gaia, shoving her, pushing her, tripping her until she fell to the ground. It was beautiful. Her daughter was perfect. She ran to join her in the wide, pebbly open space, surrounded only by looming warehouse buildings.

By the time she got there, Tatiana was on the ground, straddling Gaia, her hands in a choking stranglehold around her neck. Gaia's arms were flailing, smacking haphazardly at Tatiana's face, shoulders, anywhere, just trying to get a grip on her to defend herself. But it was useless. Natasha approached and placed a foot squarely in the center of Gaia's chest, making it impossible for Gaia to move. Tatiana let go of her throat and held her flailing arms to the ground.

"Natasha," she wheezed, unable to get a decent breath with a boot on her chest. "Why are you doing this?"

"Stop the charade," Natasha scolded her. "I think you were expecting to see us. Perhaps not tonight, in this place, but when you took our gun, you knew we would come after you."

"Yeah, it was a big surprise," Gaia answered from her prone position. "Finding out you were double crossing me and my father after all. So tell me—do you get paid well for being a whore?"

"Shut up, you bitch," Tatiana screeched. She spit in Gaia's face. Gaia flinched but couldn't turn away; her hair, stuck under her shoulders, kept her head pinned helplessly.

Natasha gave a deep, throaty laugh. "My daughter is very protective of me," she said. "It is the kind of trait you find in families. Oh, but you wouldn't know anything about that, would you, my little orphan?"

"I'm not an orphan," Gaia seethed. "I'm going to find my father."

Natasha's face darkened, and her smile turned to steel.

"The only place you'll find him is in hell, when I send you there," she said.

Gaia's eyes widened. Natasha could see her expression change even in the dim moonlight. She gave an incredulous stare.

"You're a liar," she said. "You're a bitch and a liar. My father's not dead."

"Oh, but he is," Natasha wheedled, in a parody of the soothing voice she used to use to comfort Gaia. "He is dead. I fed him poison at that dinner myself. I watched him choke and hoped he wouldn't make it to the hospital. And I worked with our agents to have him disappear from under the doctors' noses. He's gone, Gaia. Deep under the East River by now."

Gaia seemed paralyzed. She glared at Natasha, weighing the truth in this statement.

"It's terrible," Tatiana taunted her. "If anything happened to my mother, I would know immediately. And I certainly would find her and protect her if she was in danger. But you? You just let your father die. You did nothing."

Gaia roared and bucked her body backward. The convulsive movement caught Natasha off guard and she reeled backward, momentarily off balance. Gaia punched and kicked at her wildly, then turned and ran back toward the water towers, running toward the gap between them.

"Coward!" Natasha called after her. She gave chase, galloping after Gaia, Tatiana lagging behind. This was becoming tiring. Amusing as it was to tease this pathetic creature, Natasha wanted to silence her once and for all. Perhaps with a twist of the head to break her neck. Perhaps with the long, thin weapon she had tucked into her boot. But first she had to catch the stupid girl yet again. She saw her disappear around the right tower, but she was right behind. She rounded the tower and saw—

Ha!

A dizzying halogen light splashed into her vision. Her pupils ached as they tried to dilate in the sudden flash. But before she could figure out where it was coming from, arms grabbed her from every direction, knocking her backward, shoving her against the metal side of the tower.

Ambushed? Attacked?

Impossible!

Unless. . .

"Gaia!" she shrieked. "It's impossible. I'm supposed to kill you! What did you do? Who are these people?"

"CIA," she heard Gaia's voice tell her from somewhere in the gloom beyond the spotlight.

Natasha fought. With every fiber of her being she lashed out against the black-clad men who had her pinned from every angle. All her satisfaction, all her anticipation turned to horrified dread and the sickening realization that she'd been had.

"The phone call. You knew," she snarled. "Oh, you think you are so clever. You little bitch, I'm so glad I killed your father. Do you know he died begging to see you again?"

"Shut her up," Gaia's voice snapped. Natasha heard footsteps crunching away.

"You can't shut me up," Natasha screamed after her. "You'll hear me in your dreams, Gaia. You'll hear me and see me and you'll never forget how you loved me. Me, Gaia. The woman who killed Thomas Moore!"

Natasha felt her windpipe being squeezed by the leather-clad hand of a CIA operative. She gave a strangled shout and felt a flash of pain behind her eyes as she gasped for breath. A moment later she could breathe again as she was thrown bodily into the back of a paddy wagon. She struggled to stand and look out the back window. Then she began pounding on the doors.

195

Pounding. First slowly. Then quickly. Pounding in time with the wild beating of her heart. Fury ripping through her veins as she saw her prize snatched from her grasp with one stupid voice mail. She could kill herself for this. So anxious to close the deal, she hadn't seen the glaringly obvious fact that she was being set up.

"Gaia!" she screamed. "Gaia! GAAAIAAAA!"

TATIANA SAW THE BURST OF LIGHT

Instincts

as Natasha was captured and stepped backward into the shadows. She watched her mother, her beautiful, proud mother, captured by thugs and treated like a common streetwalker. She nearly leapt into the light to join her mother in battling the attackers. But something stopped her. Almost like a hand, reaching out and pulling her back.

Stop. Something told her. *Someone.* It was her mother's voice, speaking from her heart.

What is the logical progression if I run to help her? that part of Tatiana asked.

I'll fight, but I'll get captured, too. There are too many of them, she answered inwardly.

Then run.

With the instincts Natasha had instilled in her, Tatiana cut her losses and turned her back on her mother. It was the most wrenching thing she had ever done. But that voice inside her had spoken the truth. What good was she to her mother from inside a prison cell?

Tatiana could hear the shouts of the government agents behind her. Looking for her. Clumsy men. Fools. If she hadn't been concentrating so hard on slipping, invisible, into the streets of Brooklyn, Tatiana would have laughed.

But there would be plenty of time for laughter after she crossed the water. She'd use whatever she had to use to get back to Manhattan and contact the people who would help her.

Then she'd laugh. And she'd wait. Wait to get her revenge on Gaia. For trapping her mother. For taking her place. And just—just for being Gaia.

Then Tatiana would laugh like hell.

Rivulets of Dread

"DMITRI," GAIA CALLED OUT AS SHE stormed away from Natasha. "Where's Dmitri?" she asked one of the big CIA guys. He ignored her. She caught another one by the arm.

"I'm looking for Dmitri," she said.

He barked into a walkie-talkie. "We need to find the daughter," he told someone. "Excuse me," he said to Gaia, shaking her off as he ran to round up Tatiana.

Gaia felt sick and desperate. And cold inside. She had to know. She'd been told her father was dead before, but this—coming from someone so close— Natasha really seemed to know. Rivulets of dread snaked through her heart as she made her way back to the caravan of cars and vans hidden behind a warehouse. A huge square light created daylight on the deserted street. It was like a movie set. Only this was real life, and Gaia had to find out the ending. Now.

Then she saw him. Dmitri. Standing off to the side, eerily still among all the activity. Dressed in black, his close-cropped gray-haired head pale in the light, he stared at her from across the street. She met his eyes and felt drawn toward him. She stopped running and walked, her stride even and purposeful, willing the space between them to shrink more quickly with each step.

"It's not true, right?" she asked, stopping a foot away from him.

He just gazed back at her, his eyes impossibly sad, the blue of them as open and endless as a noontime sky over a freshly dug grave.

"Dmitri. Is it true?"

He shook his head. "We don't know," he said. "There is no way we can be sure. Given what we know about Natasha, it's definitely possible."

Gaia knew Natasha could be lying. She'd seen her father rise from the dead more than once. But the possibility of it made her tired. Exhausted, in fact. Like her heart was made of granite. If it were true, then she had totally failed him. And if it weren't true? She wasn't any closer to finding him than she had been the night he disappeared. It was all too much.

She didn't know if she took the last step toward the old man or if he moved toward her, but Gaia felt his arms fold around her as she closed her eyes and stood trembling with confusion, allowing herself for one brief moment to feel the comfort of another human being. She'd searched so long for her father—wasted so many years hating him when she should have just been glad he was alive. Glad to share a planet with him. And when she was supposed to be watching out for him, she'd lived nose to nose with his wanna-be murderers, never lifting a finger to help him. Guilt turned her insides to custard. She thought she'd die of this feeling. The only thing that would ease the pain was her father. Her father. And she was farther away from him than ever.

And after all he'd done for her, she'd been so inept and useless—it was as bad as if she'd tried to murder him herself.

It was a touching sight, the young mournful girl in the old man's arms. Gaia barely noticed when Natasha's paddy wagon started up and drove past her and Dmitri down the artificially lit street. But

Natasha's face gazed dispassionately from the window. Watched Gaia as she pulled away. Receded as the truck gained speed. Soon she was nothing but a speck in a tiny rectangle of light, disappearing down the dark, desolate streets of Brooklyn.

here is a sneak peek of Fearless™ #28: CHASE

Around every
corner she
passed
could be
the gun that
held the
bullet that
would end
her life.

no

place

else

to

go

IT WASN'T A UNIQUE EXPERIENCE

Gooey Gaze

for Gaia Moore, wandering the streets of New York City with nowhere to go. It wasn't even a unique experience for her to believe that her father was dead, that she was next, that around every corner she passed could be the gun that held the bullet that would end her life. It was just that it had been so long since she had been so entirely alone. Weeks, even. Months.

There was no one left.

Gaia pulled her collar up against the cold breeze that blew harder and more bitingly with each passing moment. It was late spring, but then, Manhattan never seemed to adhere to the *Farmer's Almanac*. The island had taken on the general attitude of its inhabitants and had mastered the ability to give an "Up yours!" to even the likes of Mother Nature. At least it kept the throngs of people off the streets and inside, watching their rented movies and eating their delivery food. Fewer innocents for Gaia to trample. She turned a corner and bent into the wind.

Just above the soft, worn cotton of her jacket, Gaia made sure her eyes were free and peeled. Natasha had been captured and was now in the custody of the CIA. At this very moment she was being questioned, interrogated, maybe even beaten (one could dream). But

Tatiana was still out there somewhere. She could be anywhere. And she still had orders to kill Gaia.

Not if I kill you first, Gaia thought, her rage bubbling over from her heart into her thoughts. It was still hard to swallow, the fact that Tatiana was in on it. The fact that everything they'd been through together had been a lie. That she'd actually been snowed by a little blond DKNY-sporting fake.

"It doesn't matter," Gaia spoke into the collar of her jacket, her warm breath heating her cheeks and mouth. So she'd lost Tatiana. Big deal. She'd lost more important people in her lifetime. Much more important. And if she bumped into the girl right now, she'd kick the crap out of her first and ask questions later. One question, actually. The only one that mattered.

Where is my father?

Yes, Natasha had claimed that he was dead. And Gaia had no reason to not believe her. Except, of course, that everything else the woman had ever said or done had been a lie. At this point, she gave her father a 50-50 chance of still being down with the breathing folk. But she was 100 percent sure that Tatiana knew the truth. And those were good odds to be working with.

If she only knew where the hell the girl was.

"All alone, no place to go, all alone, no place to go."

Gaia paused for a moment, taken off guard by the rambling words of the homeless man who was suddenly blocking her path. He looked at her with wild, blank eyes, shaking a battered blue-and-white coffee cup in front of her, the piddling change inside rattling pathetically. He was bundled inside about four flannel coats but somehow still looked impossibly cold. He shuffled toward her, his gooey gaze settling somewhere around the bridge of her nose.

"All alone, no place to go, all alone, no place to go. . ."

She knew he was just one of the thousands of unlucky people who had been driven insane by life on the street, but for a moment it felt as if he were` looking right through her skin into her heart. Somehow he was extracting the exact words she was trying to keep from eating away at her.

"All alone, no place to go, all alone, no place to go. . ."

"All right, all right!" Gaia said. She stuffed her hand into the depths of her jeans pocket and came out with a quarter. "Here," she said, tossing the coin into the cup. The man didn't acknowledge it—he simply took up the refrain once more.

"All alone, no place to go, all alone, no place to go. . ."

Gaia started to run.

She ran to feel the wind on her face, to get her blood pumping, to hear the roar of the cars and people passing by in her ears, to drown out the man's ceaseless words.

"All alone, no place to go, all alone, no place to go. . ."

She didn't even realize that she was headed for Ed's building until she was standing right in front of it. The tears that had been torn from her eyes by the stinging wind as she ran made little streaks across her temples, tightening the skin. Gaia sucked in a breath and pulled her jacket closer. She stared at the door.

This was it. This was the place she always used to be able to come to when there was no place else to go. Ed was the one person who had always been there for her, without fail. But she'd screwed that up too, hadn't she? She'd screwed everything up.

Trying not to think about the comfort that lay just beyond those sleek glass doors, Gaia turned her steps toward Washington Square Park. It was time to admit the inevitable. If she was going to get any rest tonight, which she'd need if she was going to track down Tatiana, then she was going to have to scare herself up a park bench. Washington Square Park was downtown's Motel 6 for runaways and druggies. The only difference was that a person didn't need to lay out any cash to get a bed.

Gaia slipped into the park by the West entrance and started along the circle. A large woman dozed sitting up on the first bench, surrounded by dozens of shopping bags full of clothing and rags and heaven only knew what else. There was a shopping cart tied to the bench with a red bandana, and a kitten was curled up in the child's seat among a bunch of tangled scarves. On the next bench was a scrawny kid with barely enough clothing on to keep him comfortable on a hot summer's day, shivering away even as he slept. Gaia averted her eyes and choked back her pity. He was probably an addict who had left a perfectly good home behind him somewhere, and at that moment, Gaia couldn't feel sorry for him. All she could think about was the warm bed out there with his name on it.

Finally, Gaia came across an empty bench. She glanced around to make sure the immediate area was creep free. Satisfied, she laid down, her face toward the back of the seat, and curled her arm under her head.

Don't think about anything, she told herself. *You can deal with it all tomorrow.*

As Gaia felt herself starting to drift, she silently thanked the stars for her ability to fall asleep anywhere. But just as her thoughts were fading to black, the entire bench shook from the force of a powerful blow. She sat up straight and looked right into the stubble-covered face of a square-shouldered, square-jawed, totally strung-out junkie. His eyes were rimmed with red and his breathing was ragged. He bared his teeth like a rabid dog.

"This is my bench, girlie," he said, gracing Gaia with a cloud of breath that smelled of rotten beer.

"Leave me alone," Gaia said, starting to lie down again. She was definitely not in the mood.

The junkie walked around to the front of the bench, grabbed the back of Gaia's jacket, and yanked her to the ground. Her shoulder hit the asphalt and her head bounced against the hard ground. Quickly, Gaia rolled over onto her stomach and pushed herself up. When she turned around, the junkie was right in her face, laughing. Gaia scrunched up her nose and tried not to breathe.

"Look, when I got here, the bench was empty," Gaia said. "You don't look like the brightest guy in the world, but I'm sure you've heard of finders keepers."

" 'F you won't give the bench up, I got no problem takin' it from ya," the guy said.

Gaia rolled her eyes. For once, she didn't feel like fighting, but she'd already had more than enough of the grandstanding banter portion of the evening. She had a feeling that this was the type of guy who could stand here and trade threats until he passed out, but there was no telling how long that would take. Besides, the sweet taste of sleep was still in her mouth and she wanted to get back there. So she decided to take the short cut. She reached out and shoved him.

The junkie staggered back, surprised, then narrowed his eyes and threw a wide, arcing punch. Gaia easily blocked it, grasped his arm and turned into him, jabbing her elbow back into his stomach. He doubled over slightly, and she brought her skull back into his with a crack. When she spun away from him and took her fighting stance, he already looked pretty beaten up. Gaia was about to let her guard down when he let out a battle cry and rushed her, tackling her right to the ground.

Gaia tried to push him off of her, waiting for her adrenaline to kick in, waiting for that rush of energy, but it didn't come. She was just tired. And not a little bit bored. As she contemplated this, the junkie got one good punch into her gut and another to her jaw that sent stars across her vision. Gaia had had enough. She propped her calves under his torso and lifted, flipping him up and over her head, onto his back. He let out a groan as he fell. Gaia got up and hovered over him.

"Are we done yet?" she asked.

He waved his hands in front of his face and winced. "We're done! We're done! Please don't hurt me!"

"Fine," Gaia said, trying not to show how relieved she was. "Just get the hell out of here."

The junkie stood up, keeping his distance from Gaia, then ran off awkwardly into the night. Gaia trudged back over to her bench, feeling heavy and low and disappointed. She couldn't remember the last time she hadn't gotten worked up and focused and generally jazzed during a fight. And right now she felt about as alive as she did in her highly unstimulating math class every day. What was wrong with her? It wasn't like she hadn't been in places as depressing as this before. She'd spent almost her entire life in them.

But this time was somehow different. When she reached inside and tried to summon up some kind of motivating emotion—anger, vengefulness—all she felt was. . . broken.

She laid down on the bench again, her brow furrowing as she put her head down on the pillow of her bent arm.

Don't think about anything, she told herself again. *You can deal with it all tomorrow.*

Then she closed her eyes and let sleep finally come.

TATIANA'S HAND SHOOK VIOLENTLY AS she attempted for the third time to master the simple act of inserting a key into a lock. She blamed her shivering on the fact that she hadn't expected the sudden shift in the weather and so hadn't dressed for it. She also hadn't expected, however, to see her mother get dragged off by a couple of huge men in black spy gear.

Bitch On A Mission

"Damn it. Get a grip," she said through her teeth. If her mother could see her now, she'd be ashamed. Tatiana had to pull herself together. Her mother was counting on her.

Finally, Tatiana gripped her right hand with her left to steady it, and mercifully, the key slid into the lock. There was a moment of suspense as she turned it, but the lock clicked and the door swung open with a slow, angry creak as if it had just been woken from a deep slumber. Tatiana had the right place. She was home.

She slipped through the door and quickly punched the code her mother had made her memorize into the key pad on the near wall, the red light flashing menacingly as she worked. After hitting all the numbers, Tatiana pressed her thumb into the enter key and squeezed her eyes shut. The alarm let out a loud beep, and when she opened her eyes again, the red light had turned to green. Tatiana closed the door behind her and fastened all five safety locks. She leaned back against the door and allowed herself to breathe. She was safe. Alone, but safe.

Peeling off her lightweight jacket, Tatiana decided to explore her new abode. In the semidarkness she found a light switch and flicked it on, illuminating the small living room with the weak light from a single overhead fixture. She'd been hearing about the Alphabet City safe house ever since she and her mother had arrived in New York City, but she'd never been here. The moment she saw the place in the light, she felt an almost painful longing for the lofty space of the Seventy-second Street apartment.

Your mother is most likely in a jail cell right now, she told herself. *Quit your whining.*

She breathed in the musty, sooty smell of the air and took a few steps into the tiny square living room. The walls where plain and white, and an old but comfortable-looking corduroy couch stood to one side. A table next to it held a single glass lamp with a dingy

11

shade. Tatiana walked over to the one piece of artwork on the wall—a framed print of Renoir's "The Luncheon of the Boating Party," and lifted it from the nail that held it in place. Just as she'd been told, there was a square gray safe door built into the wall. Tatiana quickly dialed in the combination, which she'd also committed to memory, and the door popped open, letting out a hiss of air.

There were stacks upon stacks of bills inside— American dollars, Canadian dollars, Mexican pesos, British pounds, and Russian rubles. Tatiana slipped a few twenties from one of the bundles of dollars, then pulled out a stack of passports. As she flipped through them—there were at least ten with her picture, each from a different country— she smirked sadly at the names her mother had given her. Annie Whitmore, Corrine Deveneaux, Marianna Alonso, Marcella Tuscano.

I could just disappear, Tatiana thought, allowing the seduction of such a thought to momentarily wet her lips and send her pulse racing. She gazed at her picture in the Italian passport and imagined it—imagined herself on the white sands of the Mediterranean, sipping something fruity and letting her bare back bathe in the sun. But as quickly as the image came, she squelched it. She wasn't going anywhere without her mother. Not now. Not ever.

She took the last items out of the safe, a nice, sleek

.45 pistol and a full clip, then shoved the passports back inside. She shoved the clip into the gun, savoring the menacing click as it locked into place. After making sure the safety was on, Tatiana slipped the gun between her waistband and her back. Then she closed the safe and hung the painting again. She had to check the rest of her provisions.

The kitchen, just to the left of the living room, was lined with avocado green cabinets and held a large brown refrigerator. Tatiana walked over to the pantry and checked inside. The shelves were stocked with canned soups, pasta sauces, packets of instant oatmeal, and cans of soda and juice.

She walked back across the living room to the bedroom, which took all of three steps, and flicked on the light. Two twin-size beds, draped with blue blankets, stood on either side of a single nightstand. Inspection of a small dresser against the far wall revealed drawers filled with plain underwear, bras, T-shirts and sweaters in Tatiana and Natasha's sizes. The closet held a few pairs of jeans, assorted footwear and two heavy winter coats. On the top shelf was a wide array of wigs, hats and sunglasses. Tatiana pulled down a long, dark wig with natural-looking waves and smiled morosely. Her mother had certainly been prepared.

She just hadn't been prepared to be double-crossed by Gaia Moore.

Still fingering the coarse hair of the wig, Tatiana sat

down on the closest bed and tried to remain calm. She tried to stop herself from picturing the events of the evening over and over and over again. Reliving the nightmare was not going to help her deal with it. It wasn't going to bring her mother back to her. There was only one thing that would. She had to make Gaia talk. Gaia was the only person who knew where her mother was—who knew who the men were that had taken her.

From their uniform fighting tactics, it was clear they belonged to some government agency, and considering Tom Moore's affiliation with the CIA, Tatiana assumed it was them. But that meant nothing to her. It wasn't as if she were privy to all the CIA's secret interrogation facilities. As much as she hated to admit it, she needed Gaia. Unfortunately, she knew that the self-righteous, egotistical bitch on a mission was never going to help her.

What Tatiana needed was a plan.

Taking a deep breath, she gathered her blond hair up on top of her head and pulled the wig on over it. It was tight, but all the better. She tugged at the temples, then walked over to the full-length mirror that was attached to the back of the door, suddenly hyperaware of the cold steel against the skin of her back. When she saw her reflection, she smiled slowly. It was perfect—a total transformation.

Tatiana pulled her gun out of her waistband,

hoisted it, and aimed it at her reflection, her arms straight and locked at the elbow. She barely even recognized herself. Tatiana smirked, brought the gun to her mouth and blew across the tip of the barrel. Whatever her plan might turn out to be, Gaia would never see her coming.

Aaron Corbet isn't a bad kid—he's just a little different.

On the eve of his eighteenth birthday, Aaron is dreaming of a darkly violent landscape. He can hear the sounds of weapons clanging, the screams of the stricken, and another sound that he cannot quite decipher. But as he gazes upward to the sky, he suddenly understands. It is the sound of great wings beating the air unmercifully as hundreds of armored warriors descend on the battlefield.

The flapping of angels' wings.

Orphaned since birth, Aaron is suddenly discovering newfound—and sometimes supernatural—talents. But not until he is approached by two men does he learn the truth about his destiny—and his own role as a liaison between angels, mortals, and Powers both good and evil—some of whom are bent on his own destruction....

the
fallen

a new series by Thomas E. Sniegoski

Book One available March 2003

From Simon Pulse

Published by Simon & Schuster

AN AGELESS VENDETTA, AN ETERNAL LOVE, AND A DEADLY POWER . . .

"I'm living in a new town with a new family, and suddenly I'm discovering new powers, having new experiences, and meeting all sorts of new people. Including Jer. So why does it feel like I've known him forever? Even before I was born? It's almost like . . . magic."

WICKED

A new series about star-crossed lovers
from rival witch families

Book One: **WITCH**
Book Two: **CURSE**
Book Three: **LEGACY**

Available From Simon Pulse